CROSS
STITCH

CROSS STITCH

A Quilters Club Mystery

Marjory Sorrell
Rockwell

ABSOLUTELY AMAZING eBOOKS

ABSOLUTELY AMAZING eBOOKS

Published by Whiz Bang LLC, 926 Truman Avenue, Key West, Florida 33040, USA.

For information contact:
Publisher@AbsolutelyAmazingEbooks.com

ISBN-13: 978-1945772566 (Absolutely Amazing Ebooks)
ISBN-10: 1945772565

"I would rather be a superb meteor, every atom of me in magnificent glow, than a sleepy and permanent planet."

         - Jack London

Other Quilters Club Mysteries
By Marjory Sorrell Rockwell

A Christmas Quit (Prequel)

The Quilters Club Quartet

The Underhanded Stitch

The Patchwork Puzzler

Coming Unraveled

Hemmed In

Sewed Up Tight

All Tangled Up

Needled

A Stitch In Time

Available from
AbsolutelyAmazingEbooks.com

CROSS STITCH

PART ONE

The Meteorite

"My dad took me out to see a meteor shower when I was a little kid, and it was scary for me because he woke me up in the middle of the night. My heart was beating; I didn't know what he wanted to do. He wouldn't tell me, and he put me in the car and we went off, and I saw all these people lying on blankets, looking up at the sky."

- Steven Spielberg

CHAPTER ONE

The Fireball

In the Fall of 1896 a meteorite landed in a field ten miles outside of Caruthers Corners, Indiana. It was discovered by a farm boy named Beauregard Madison. He had seen it streak across the sky, a fireball that made an odd hissing sound. At the time he'd been about a quarter-mile away, looking for a stray cow named Blue Belle. He swore that the ground shook from the meteorite's impact.

Beau located the small crater without much effort, for it landed near his father's grain silo. The stone structure had been damaged by the space object's downward trajectory. Knocked it right over. The darkened round object he found was no bigger than a Chicago-style softball. There it lay, at the center of a deep impression in the ground, like an egg in a nest.

To young Beau Madison's amazement, the meteorite wasn't hot to the touch, even though he'd witnessed its fiery descent. A simple country boy, he knew nothing about astrophysics: Meteoroids enter the earth's atmosphere at very high speeds (25,000 to 160,000 MPH), but similar to firing a bullet into water a meteoroid rapidly decelerates as it penetrates the atmosphere. This drag causes the meteoroid to lose much of its velocity while still several miles up. At this retardation point, it begins to accelerate again at 32 feet per second squared due to the pull of gravity. The meteorite quickly reaches a terminal velocity of 200 to 400 MPH before impacting the ground. During this final free-fall, the meteorite experiences very little frictional heating and often reaches the ground at a temperature only slightly above the ambient atmosphere.

Beau Madison picked up the rock with its blackened crust and hefted it in his hand. Not heavy, about ten pounds at most. He carried it home and set it on the dresser next to his bed.

~ ~ ~

In 2017 the so-called Madison Meteorite would be a prime attraction at the Caruthers Corners Historical Society, placed on display in the Society's wing of the Perricock Museum of Science & History. The new museum can be found up there on High Jinks Hill, overlooking the patchwork pattern of the small Indiana town.

The meteorite had been donated to the Society by Beauregard Hollingsworth Madison IV, the now 60-year-old son of that 14-year-old boy who'd discovered the space rock.

Legend had it the meteorite killed a man when it landed, but the current Beau Madison refused to talk about that. What actually took place remains a family secret.

That was about to change. But it would take a murder to make it happen.

CHAPTER TWO

Family Heirloom

Maddy Madison had encouraged her husband to turn the meteorite over to the Historical Society. For as long as she could remember it had gathered dust on the bookshelf in their den, a curiosity piece that simply took up space.

"But it's a family heirloom," Beau protested. "A genuine falling star."

"So make a wish on it ... then kiss that grimy old rock goodbye, dear."

"But it's been in the family for years. Beau Three found this piece of space rubble after it shot like a bullet through the roof of the farm's silo." He was referring to his father, but in the Madison family, patriarchs were tracked by number.

"Yes, I've heard the story a thousand times," Maddy waved his words away.

"You don't understand," he argued. "In all the world there exist fewer than 1,200 specimens of witnessed meteorite falls. I looked it up."

"That's why people would want to see it on display at the Historical Society. It's your duty to share this rare treasure with the public."

"But —"

"You'd have naming rights. You could name it after your father."

"Well, that's a thought," he'd acquiesced.

~ ~ ~

Meteorites are usually named for the place they're found. The Meteoritical Society – made up of over 1,000 scientists and amateur enthusiasts from more than 40 countries – publishes "Guidelines For Meteorite Nomenclature." It suggests, "A new meteorite shall be named after a geographical locality near to the location of its initial recovery."

However, as owner of the meteorite that landed near Caruthers Corners, Beau Madison had insisted it be named after his father rather than the town. That was a condition of his donating it to the Historical Society. And that's how you'll find it listed in the "Catalogue of Meteorites," a registry for all known meteorites and their various pieces.

~ ~ ~

For the past decade Cookie Bentley had served as executive director of the Caruthers Corners Historical Society. She was one of Maddy's best friends. Cookie had been after the meteorite for years. Beau's donation was a great coup, the perfect opening exhibit for the organization's new home in a wing of the Perricock Museum of Science & History. No doubt people would come from as far as Indianapolis to see this historic artifact.

Beau's meteorite was unique in several ways. First, it had been sighted and found – what's called a "meteorite fall." That's rare. Second, it was a fireball.

According to the American Meteor Society, "Most of our current knowledge about the origin of meteoroids comes from photographic fireball studies (meteors > magnitude -4) done over the last 50 years or so. This may sound like a long time, but good data has been collected on only about 800 fireballs so far. Of these, only 4 have been recovered on the ground as meteorites. A meteorite-causing fireball is very rare and must be at least magnitude -8 to have sufficient mass to survive the trip. Even with an accurate photographic or video trajectory, it is still a matter of finding a needle in a haystack once the meteorite is on the ground."

Cookie was well aware of this uniqueness. She had been talking with Dr. Archimedes L. Claypool in the Astronomy Department at the University of Indiana Bloomington. Home of the historic Kirkwood Observatory and its 12-inch refracting telescope, the university offered a doctoral program that has produced over 100 Ph.D. astronomers now engaged in teaching and research worldwide. Dr. Claypool had agreed to be guest speaker for the opening of an exhibit of the famed Madison Meteorite.

Obtaining good information about meteorites is difficult, due to the limited number of professional texts in this field. Fortunately, Dr. Claypool was author of *Meteor Science and Celestial Observations*, a respected study used in many college classrooms.

In fact, his textbook had devoted an entire paragraph to this particular meteorite:

In 1896 during a November meteor shower, a chondrite meteorite weighing 10- or 11-lb. landed near Caruthers Corners, a small town in northeastern Indiana. Not much is known about this specimen, for it has been closely held by the family of the young farm boy who found it. The meteorite reportedly measures about 5 inches in diameter and has a blackish-brown appearance. Aerolites (i.e. stony meteorites composed mainly of silicates) comprise about 69 per cent of all known specimens.

Yes, Dr. Claypool would be the perfect lecturer to introduce the first public appearance of the Madison Meteorite.

CHAPTER THREE

Meet the Quilters Club

Madelyn Madison headed a group of local women who called themselves the Quilters Club. They met each Tuesday at the Hoosier State Senior Recreational Center to work on patchwork quilts. They had won a number of prizes in the quilting competition at the annual Watermelon Days festival.

There were only five members – Maddy, Cookie, Bootsie, Lizzie, and young Aggie. Six, if you counted Aggie's cousin N'yen, a prepubescent whiz kid who had no interest in quiltmaking ... but liked to help them solve mysteries.

The Quilters Club had earned the reputation of being amateur detectives. The women had solved several local mysteries – ranging from circus boys who got lost in Never Ending Swamp to a mad scientist who tried to poison the town's water supply, from unmasking the "ghost" of Beasley Manor to catching the thieves who tried to steal Capt. Perceval Perricock's antediluvian fossil collection.

Fourteen-year-old Aggie and twelve-year-old N'yen were eldest among Beau and Maddy's five grandchildren. Hard to believe the family had expanded so fast. Of them, N'yen and his little cousin Donna Ann were adopted. But so was Maddy.

After recently discovering she was the secret love child of one of the town's famous Hoople Quadruplets,

Maddy had come into a fat trust fund. That windfall allowed her to buy a new pumper truck for the Caruthers Corners Fire Department (where her son Freddie was Fire Chief); give a large donation to a non-profit children's service in Chicago (that her son Bill ran); and put a new roof on the town hall (where her son-in-law Mark served as Mayor). Also, she established a college fund for each of her five grandchildren. Plus: Aggie and N'yen got new GT Grade Carbon Ultegra 11-Speed road bikes.

Everybody won!

Even Aggie's dog Tige got a new supply of soup bones. His favorite.

Beauregard Madison paid little attention to the fact that his wife was now wealthy. They still lived in their modest Victorian home on Melon Pickers Row. Still drove the 2015 Toyota Sequoia with 80,000 miles on it. Still made do with that old Weber gas grill on the back patio. Still used cents-off coupons when shopping at Food Lion.

And Beau still went fishing on weekends with his grandson N'yen and Lizzie's husband Edgar Ridenour – relentlessly pursuing their quest to hook an elusive catfish known as Big Calvin. The chucklehead was said to lurk near the bridge where Highway 101 crosses over the Wabash River.

~ ~ ~

Although Beau Madison remained mum on the subject, Cookie Bentley was determined to chase down the truth behind that legend about the Madison Meteorite killing a bystander when it crashed to earth in 1896.

A History of Caruthers Corners and Surrounding Environs by Martin J. Caruthers had stated only this:

"In 1896 a fiery celestial missile struck the ground outside of town, reportedly killing a local farm boy. No more is known of the story."

If true, there must some sort of death certificate ... or record of a missing person.

The idea fascinated Cookie. After all, someone being killed by a meteorite is all but unheard of. Even though thousands of meteors pass through the earth's atmosphere every single day, the vast majority burn up before landing. Of those that actually make it to earth, most come down over oceans or uninhabited regions. Many end up falling into the sea, unnoticed. The chances of one striking someone is ... well, astronomical.

Last year marked "the first time in recorded history a meteorite is reported to have killed a person," claimed a news report Cookie found on Google. Crashing onto a college campus in southern India, it supposedly killed a bus driver and injured three others. However, NASA scientists issued a public statement saying that photographs of the event were more consistent with "a land based explosion" than something from space.

The most famous case in the US occurred in 1954, when Ann Hodges of Sylacauga, Alabama, was hit by a space rock while napping on her couch. She wasn't seriously injured. Photographs show a large bruise covering the left side of her body.

In 2003 a huge comet exploded above central

Russia, injuring 1,200 people. Exhibiting a force 30 times that of the Hiroshima bomb, it caused $33 million in property damage. But no deaths.

A Tulane University professor calculated the odds of dying by the impact of a meteorite as 1 in 1,600,000. Compare that with 1 in 90 for a car accident, 1 in 250 for a fire, 1 in 60,000 for a tornado, and 1 in 135,000 for lightning. Not a likely occurrence.

"You have a better chance of getting hit by a tornado and a bolt of lightning and a hurricane all at the same time," noted one wry astronomer.

Still, the rumor about a man being killed by the Madison Meteorite was persistent. Granny Crackleton swore Beau Madison III told her about it.

~ ~ ~

Maddy Madison had tried to worm the truth out of her husband, but he refused to talk about the meteorite. "Leave the past undisturbed," he offered his polite refusal.

Nonetheless, she conspired with her pal Cookie to get to the bottom of this long-ago meteorite business. Their fellow Quilters Clubbers agreed to help. After all, wasn't this a mystery to be solved?

Besides, there happened to be a quilting tie-in. Inside the Indiana State Museum hangs a patchwork quilt depicting the 1896 landing of the meteorite. The quilt had been handsewn by Beau's grandmother, Mary Louise Madison. Based on her son's eyewitness description, it is the only "contemporaneous record" of this important astronomical event. Everything else is solely hearsay, aside from the *prima facie* evidence of the meteorite itself.

Known as a Pictorial Quilt, the design shows a shooting star, a tall farm silo, and a boy on the ground staring upward at the approaching meteorite. It's quite colorful, as unfaded as the day Mary Louise stitched the bright fabric swatches together in 1898, two years after the event.

Beau Four traced his lineage back to the town's founders – Col. Beauregard Hollingsworth Madison, Jacob Abernathy Caruthers, and Ferdinand Aloysius Jinks. The trio had been leading a wagon train west in 1829 when a broken wheel encouraged them to settle here on the banks of the Wabash River. To the chagrin of Beau Madison and Ferdie Jinks, the outpost got named after that self-aggrandizing rapscallion, Jacob Caruthers. Their descendants had quarreled over this inequity for years.

By insisting that the meteorite be named after its discoverer, Beau felt that he was preserving the family's name in local history. To heck with the Caruthers and Jinks lineages.

~ ~ ~

The Quilters Club gals were all prominent citizens of Caruthers Corners. Maddy's hubby was a former mayor and namesake of one of the town founders; Cookie, the historian married to a successful farmer named Ben Bentley; Bootsie, wife of Police Chief Jim Purdue; and Lizzie, spouse of retired bank president Edgar Ridenour.

Aggie and N'yen rounded out the quilting bee's numbers. After the split of his adoptive parents, N'yen now lived with his grandparents. His cousin Aggie resided only a few streets away in a big house on the town square. The two were inseparable.

Currently, the Quilters Club was working on a group project, a Community Quilt for Willamina Haney, a local lady suffering from Stage IV cancer. Her death had been long expected, but she managed to linger on like a guest not quite ready to leave the party. It was felt a quilt from her friends might ease the transition.

The idea of the Community Quilt Project began four years ago with Natalie Zonker, lead singer in the choir at First Presbyterian. Natalie was gravely ill and scheduled for a surgery everyone feared she might not survive. The Quilters Club had an inspiration to make a quilt for Natalie bearing messages of love and support from the local community, encouraging words written in archival ink on muslin.

These messages were in Natalie's mind when she went into surgery. It had been successful. Thereafter, she would not enter a hospital without the quilt firmly in her arms. Last year Natalie finally succumbed to a virulent respiratory infection. Her Community Quilt commanded a place of honor at the memorial service and is now a treasured memento for her family.

Thus began a series of quilts, all based on the friendship and support of the community. The Quilters Club has made quilts for people with cancer, life-threatening infections, AIDS, kidney failure, traumatic injury, and heart problems. As Maddy put it, "These quilts are a tangible reminder that our friendship has greater power than we realize."

~ ~ ~

"Are you still trying to trace down the truth behind that old space rock?" asked Bootsie. As a policeman's wife, she didn't like the idea of a murder going unsolved – even if the culprit had been an object falling from the sky over 100 years ago.

"Yes, I am," nodded Cookie, looking up from her stitching. "Maddy's been trying to get her hubby to talk, but you know how closed-mouth Beau Madison can be."

"Like the Sphinx," nodded Lizzie, her red hair bobbing. She was the best quiltmaker among them, and had taken on the task of tutoring Aggie.

Aggie was stitching in place a muslin square that displayed the words: LIFE IS A CIRCUS, a proper sentiment for Willamina Haney who had spent her life with a traveling road show billed as **Haney Bros. Circus and Petting Zoo.** Willamina had been the "Brother" in the joint ownership with her husband, Big Bill Haney.

N'yen was sitting in a corner of the room, furiously playing GeoDefense on his iPhone. This highly tactical tower defense game is tough to beat, but the little Brainiac was working his way through the multiple levels like an electronic Sherman's March to the Sea. Without looking up or stopping his play, he said, "What's Grampy refusing to talk about? Bet I can get him to spill the beans when we go fishing on Saturday."

Aggie challenged him, "I'll bet a DQ Blizzard you can't. He's awfully tight-lipped when it comes to this particular family secret."

"But we're part of the family," argued N'yen. "He shouldn't be keeping secrets from us." Although Vietnamese by birth, the boy was fully integrated into the Madison dynasty. He'd been adopted by Maddy's son Bill and wife Kathy, but when they divorced he'd been sent to live with Grampy and Grammy. Aggie was a bit jealous.

"We may have to do our own homework on this one," counseled Maddy. "If Beauregard Madison doesn't want to talk, even an hour in an Iron Maiden wouldn't make him crack."

"What's an Iron Maiden?" asked Aggie.

"It's a Chinese torture device, first used in the Ming Dynasty," answered Cookie. She had an eidetic memory for tidbits of history. "It was like an upright coffin, filed with sharp spikes that stuck you when the door closed."

Aggie made a face. "Ugh."

"See? We Asians have our ways of making people talk," said N'yen with a sly smile. He liked playing the race card with his cousin.

"What's the story on this new mystery?" Aggie changed the topic, having had enough of torture devices and N'yen's teasing.

"Actually it's an old mystery," said Bootsie. "Goes back to your grandfather's day."

"A meteorite killed someone," explained Lizzie, pausing to check her lipstick. She was trying out a new shade called Italiano Rose. Lizzie's maiden name was Bergamachi, a remnant of her Italian heritage. Her grandfather came from Italy to start a bank in Caruthers Corners shortly after the little town sprang up in northeastern Indiana.

"That's the mystery," Maddy corrected her redheaded friend. "Whether someone was killed … or not."

"When did you say this supposedly happened?"

asked Aggie, eyes squinted dubiously.

"In 1896," answered Cookie, quick with the facts. "Your grandfather Beauregard Madison III was a witness to a meteorite crashing into a field outside of town. He recovered the 11.6-pound chunk of space debris. It is the very same meteorite we're putting on exhibit at the Historical Society next month."

"Who cares about something that happened that long ago," yawned N'yen, showing his lack of interest. He was approaching 15 million points on GeoDefense.

"Why, young man, I'm shocked," responded Cookie. "History is the bedrock of society. Without understanding the past we're due to misjudge the future."

"What's this about someone getting killed?" interjected Aggie, trying to take the heat off her cousin. She always had his back. The pair might squabble among themselves, but they were united against the rest of the world.

Maddy put down her needle. "There's an old story that the meteorite hit and killed somebody, but there's no proof of that. And your Grampy's not talking."

"How would he know?" responded N'yen. "He wasn't there in 1896."

"He has his father's diary."

Chapter Four

The False Treasury Agent

Eggie Ettelman had a scheme. If it worked, he was going to be a very, very rich man. To heck with Bobby Ray Purdue, that strutting peacock, thinking he was better than everybody else just because he was worth $100 million. What was that saying about a fool and his money?

Eggie (his birth name was Elbert Gregory Garrison Ignatius Ettelman, hence the initials E.G.G.I.E.) was claiming to be a US Treasury Agent, but the closest he'd ever come to that was once riding past the Treasury Building in Washington, DC, on a bus tour. To look the part of a government man, he'd purchased a new J.C. Penney suit and spit-polished his black shoes. His credentials came from Toys R Us, a plastic wallet with tin badge and official-looking ID card, part of a Dick Danger Detective Kit (retail price $14.95).

He had grown up in the nearby town of Burpyville, so he'd been aware of the "Lost Boys," the three kids who had disappeared into the Never Ending Swamp north of Caruthers Corners. And he'd followed the sensational events accompanying the return of Bobby Ray Purdue, after a career as a clown in the Haney Bros. Circus. But the part that interested him most was the fact that Bobby Ray had discovered a stash of Red Seal bank notes stuffed inside a family quilt. Known as Grand Watermelons (because the zeros were shaped like large watermelons), the currency was highly coveted by collectors and so by selling the rare bank notes at auction the once-upon-a-time Lost Boy became a multimillionaire.

Bobby Ray Purdue had blown nearly half his newfound wealth by setting up a home for retired circus performers and endowing a refuge for circus animals, the Haney Bros. Circus and Exotic Animal Refuge just outside of town. He'd set up a $2 million annuity to provide for his mother. Built himself a fancy house out on Melon Rind Road. Stocked his new domicile with all kinds of crazy collectibles, ranging from a stuffed Kodiak bear to a World War II Fokker D VII biplane. What's more, he'd helped fund the new Perricock Museum of Science & History as well as giving a sizable endowment to the Caruthers Corners Historical Society.

Bobby Ray Purdue had been throwing money around like a drunken Scrooge McDuck. Question was, how could Eggie Ettelman get in on this largess?

Polishing his Dick Danger Detective badge, he thought he knew just how to pull off the scam. Bobby Ray wouldn't know what hit him.

~ ~ ~

Fatty Johnson – as Cromwell Thaddeus Johnson was known – bumped into Beau Madison at the Dollar General on Main Street. Beau was there with his grandson N'yen, shopping for a present to commemorate Tét Nguyen Dan. Tét is the Vietnamese version of the Lunar New Year, an all-in-one festival that has been described as "Christmas, Thanksgiving, and your birthday all celebrated at once." In the days leading up to the weeklong holiday, Vietnamese traditionally give gifts of food to family members and friends. American-born N'yen preferred a toy.

"Beau, hold up a minute," the rotund man called out. Once a local handyman, Fatty was semi-retired after falling off a Christmas float and injuring his back a dozen or so years ago. With his white beard and rounded shape, he still looked the part of Santa Claus, but his cranky nature diminished the "jolly old elf" image.

Beau Madison turned to see who was calling. Standing there in the middle of the toy aisle, Beau held a box marked RALPH THE RADIO-CONTROLLED ROBOT. Leftover inventory from Christmas, it had been marked down to $29.95. So much for this being a dollar store. Maybe one reason the gizmo hadn't sold was it took a beanpole like Beau to fetch the box off the top shelf.

"Hi, Fatty," he acknowledged the greeting. "Haven't seen you in ages." Back when Beau owned the local Ace Hardware, he used to see the handyman on a weekly basis. In those days there hadn't been a Home Depot on the other side of town that sold hammers and nails and nuts and bolts.

"Got a favor to ask," said the man, scurrying in Beau's direction.

N'yen tugged at his grandfather's arm. "That's the robot I want. Let's go pay for it."

Beau ignored the boy's plea. "What favor you got in mind, Fatty?"

"You know how the Jinks family got passed over in *A History of Caruthers Corners and Surrounding*

Environs, that book by Martin J. Caruthers? I need your help in righting the historical record."

"Know what you mean. The Madison family got short shrift too," replied Beau, curious where this conversation was going. Whenever Fatty Johnson needed a favor, that was the time to hold onto your wallet.

"Being that I'm a direct descendant of Ferdinand Jinks on my mother's side, I've hired a writer to do a book about ol' Ferdie and his descendants. How about that?"

"Good for you. Now about that favor –?"

"I wonder if you'd let Winston Gaylord Lockwood – that's the writer's name – have a peak at your father's diary. You know, as part of his research. We want to get the facts right. Not like those lies and half-truths in the Martin Caruthers book."

Beau frowned. "No can do," he said.

"Why not? You owe it to history."

"Sorry, but Number Three – my father, that is – left instructions written on the flyleaf of his diary that its contents never be made public."

"Don't wanna make it public. I just want my writer to consult it as one of his sources. Make sure our history is accurate."

N'yen tugged at Beau's arm. "Grampy, are you gonna buy me this robot or not?" interjected the boy. Getting fidgety.

"Sure thing, N'yen. Good seeing you, Fatty."

"Wait a minute –" said Fatty Johnson as Beau followed his grandson to the front register.

Fatty only got a wave of the hand in response. Damn that arrogant Beauregard Madison! He'd get even with him.

CHAPTER FIVE

An Unexpected Visitor

"Beau, guess who dropped in for a visit," Maddy greeted her husband at the door.

"A visitor?" he said, sitting N'yen's robot box on a table in the foyer. It made a *klunk!* signifying metal parts inside.

The boy was practically jumping up and down to get at it. "Okay if I open the box?" he begged. "I want to have it programmed and working by the time Aggie comes over."

"I'm already here," his cousin announced, appearing from the kitchen. "Come meet your great uncle."

"Great uncle?" frowned N'yen.

"Do you mean Mikey?" said Beau.

Maddy spoke up, "Yes, dear, your brother Mycroft is here."

"But he's –"

"– retired in Florida?" boomed a stentorian voice. "Not anymore!" A tall figure with a lion's mane of silver hair appeared behind Aggie. He looked a lot like Beau, hair a little longer, but same features and lanky physique. "I've come home to stay, back to the town that nurtured me and gave me a plethora of wonderful memories."

"But you hated it here," blurted Beau. "That's why you left in the first place."

Mycroft Madison gave a theatrical wave of his hand. "A miscalculation on my part. I left to seek my fortune, only to discover like Dorothy in *The Wizard of Oz* that there's no place like home."

"Welcome home, Mikey," said Maddy graciously. "Where will you be staying?"

"Why, with you and my brother, of course."

That's when Beau knew Mikey had heard of his wife's inheritance, the trust fund from the Hoople Quadruplets Foundation.

~ ~ ~

Tilly hurried over to greet her uncle. She had only met Mycroft Madison once. That had been when he popped into town for Christmas, fourteen years ago. Just after the Great Snowstorm of '02. That had been the year Agnes was born.

Mycroft had gone to New York to seek his fortune. After a thirty-year career directing off-Broadway plays, he had retired to Ft. Lauderdale. Older than her dad, he must be close to 70 now. According to what her mom had said on the phone, Uncle Mikey had tired of the relentless Florida sunshine and was returning to the Hoosier state for the remainder of his "few but most glorious Golden Years." As she recalled, the man could be overly dramatic.

"Millie," he greeted his niece with open arms.

"Tilly," she politely corrected him.

"Yes, so I meant. It has been far too many years since last setting eyes on that beauteous countenance of yours."

"You've met my daughter Aggie?" she said.

"She was but a wee infant when last I was here.

22

How she's grown. I believe she's in the den with young Newton –"

"N'yen," interjected Maddy.

"– putting together a robotic monster."

"N'yen's very good at science and math," Beau said proudly.

"I'm sure he is. He has the look of genius about him. Being Asian and all."

"He's a smart kid," said Beau, looking as if he had a stomachache.

Maddy ushered everyone into the kitchen where she had a tray of newly baked watermelon tarts and a large pitcher of milk waiting. They bought their milk and butter from Old MacDonald's Dairy Farm on Cow Pasture Road. The Hitzer family (Deputy Pete's mom and dad) had owned the place for the past twenty years. It was next to the old Madison farm, land settled by Beauregard One right after that wagon train broke down in 1829. The parcel backed up to the Jinks farm; and the Caruthers spread was on the far side of that. A watermelon farmer named Boyd Aitkens owned all three tracks of land now.

"Watermelon tarts," enthused Mycroft Madison. "I remember our mother used to make them. Alas, that was over half a century ago."

"You sure you want to return to small-town life?" Beau approached the subject carefully.

"Indeed I do. Too many tourists in Ft. Lauderdale."

"What about your partner – Lawrence, that's his name, isn't it?"

"The poor bugger passed away last year. AIDS – but don't worry, I'm not infected. I've been tested recently."

"We didn't know," said Maddy. "You should have told us. We could have sent flowers. Personally Yours Flowers & Gifts is a member of TDC, I believe."

"Lawrence didn't deserve your kindness. He was unfaithful to me, as it turned out. You'd be amazed at how many young men turned up at his funeral."

"How are your sons?" Beau tried to change the subject. Talk of his brother's sexual orientation always made him uncomfortable. A touch of that Midwestern homophobia that still hung over the town like a mist.

"Matthew and Mycroft Jr. are doing fine. Have wonderful families and friends of their own. Don't need an old duffer like me hanging around."

"I'd love to meet them some day," volunteered Tilly. "Perhaps they will come visit. We could have a family reunion – the Madisons and Taylors and Hooples, all gathering here in Caruthers Corners."

"'Tis a lovely thought," said Mycroft in a way that made you know it would never happen.

CHAPTER SIX

Modern Mendacity

The *Burpyville Gazette* had been founded in 1854 by Bob Tippey's grandfather. The newspaper had been a family business up until six months ago when Bob sold the paper to the Nightley Newspapers Group.

The *Gazette* had a troubled history. It'd suspended publication from 1903 to 1914, but made a comeback with the onslaught of World War I. Its frequency had changed from daily to weekly and back several times over the years. A couple of years ago it had tried to diversify, publishing a sister paper called the *Caruthers Corners Gazette*, but that hadn't worked. The paper was no match for the Internet. Craig's List had decimated its classified advertising. Amazon had dried up retail advertising. Viewers of Fox News and CNN had quit reading the *Gazette* for politics or world events. What's more, the newspaper's reporters found steadier work at Wal-Mart and Home Depot.

Josiah Nightley was happy to have a tax write-off to help shelter profits from his big-city papers. In all, Nightley Newspapers owned 32 dailies and 14 weeklies. Also it didn't hurt that ol' Josiah owned oil wells in Oklahoma.

Over the years Bob Tippey had transferred the *Burpyville Gazette*'s archives onto microfiche. Now in the Digital Age that move looked like a poor decision, but at least these historical documents had been preserved. Newsprint is so fragile. You can imagine the tantrum Cookie Bentley threw when she learned the paper's new owner was going to dump all those dusty spools of microfiche.

Maddy Madison came to the rescue. Dipping into the new trust fund she'd received from the Hoople Quadruplets Foundation – a birthright that came when adoption papers showed she was the love child of Herbert Hoople and his inamorata Sue Ann Polk – she offered Nightley Newspapers $2,000 for the entire contents of the *Burpyville Gazette*'s Microfiche Room. Josiah Nightley was happy to take the offer. He would've been willing to give the cartons away free to anyone willing to haul them off.

Maddy immediately donated the microfiche collection to the Caruthers Corners Historical Society, and threw in a brand new microfiche reader. She got a good price ($2,450) because the company that made them was closing out the line.

"Thank you, Maddy," gushed her friend Cookie. "What can I ever do to repay you?"

"Pull out the fiche for the year 1896," she grinned.

~ ~ ~

Bootsie had volunteered to help out with the research. "Dear, how far back do your police files go?" she asked her husband. Jim Purdue had been the Caruthers Corners Chief of Police for over twenty years now.

"Why do you ask?" he said suspiciously, looking up from his morning paper. They had been enjoying a quiet breakfast of oatmeal, toast, and watermelon jam before he left for work. Being a policeman in a small

Midwestern town was not a high-pressure job.

"Cookie's looking into that old wife's tale about the Madison Meteorite killing somebody when it landed. I thought we should check the records to see if the death was reported."

"Good luck with that. All our old records are stored in the basement of the town hall, but they only go back to turn of the last century. Everything was wiped out by the Big Fire of 1899. I think the meteorite landed a few years before that."

"Oh dear. I'd forgotten. That was the fire that nearly burned down the town. Started at the First Wabash National Bank and spread like ... well, like wildfire."

"That's the one. In those days the town records were stored on the bank's upper floor. Lost them all. Birth and death records. Police reports. Property titles. The whole lot. So anything prior to 1899 is gone, destroyed by the conflagration."

"Blazes!" she cursed.

"Exactly," replied her husband, turning back to his newspaper.

~ ~ ~

Deputy Pete Hitzer was early to report in, relieving Evers Gochnauer who was back on night duty. "Anything going on?" he asked as he opened the bag of donuts he'd picked up at Cozy Café. They made them onsite. Evers already had a fresh pot of coffee going.

"Not a thing," the other deputy yawned, reaching for a maple donut. A regular routine between the two policemen.

"I hear Beau Madison's long-lost brother moved in

with him and Maddy. How long d'you think that's gonna last?"

"Five bucks says no more than two months," replied Evers, munching on the plump donut.

"I got five that says it won't last a full month," responded Petie. "I predict Beau will move that old boy out to his own place in the blink of an eye. He and Maddy were glad to get the kids out of the house."

"Yeah, but they just took in that Japanese boy."

"Vietnamese. Bill and his wife had adopted the kid before they split up."

"Bummer."

Petie finished off his two donuts. "I hear Beau's pleased as punch to have the boy living with them. Takes him fishing all the time. Edgar Ridenour goes out on the Wabash with them every weekend."

"So why not take in the brother too?" Evers reached for his second donut, not having swallowed the last bite of the first. No wonder he was slightly overweight, a problem at the annual physicals required for police officers.

"Well, I hear he's funny," said Petie.

"A comedian? I thought he was an actor. Or a director."

"No, I mean funny. Like Oliver Micherson and Jeff Brown over at Personally Yours Flowers & Gifts."

"Oh, that kinda funny," nodded Evers. "I went to school with Jeff Brown. We was on the football team together. He's a nice guy. Except for being funny."

"He ever hit on you?"

"Don't be stupid," frowned Evers. "I'm straight. Them guys are like Siamese cats. They can recognize each other in the dark. He was hardly out of high school 'fore he hooked up with Oliver. Next thing you know he was working in the flower shop."

"He's Bob Brown's brother, isn't he?"

"Right. Cookie Bentley's first husband's brother." Evers stood up and pulled on his jacket, ready to head home for a little shuteye.

"Shame about ol' Bob getting his necktie caught in that tractor wheel. Heckuva way to go. But it worked out, her marrying Ben Bentley and all."

"Well, watch me go. Beddy-bye, that is."

CHAPTER SEVEN

The Reading Room

The new microfiche reader had been delivered to the East Wing of the Perricock Museum of Science & History where the Historical Society was now located. Extensive renovation had provided two exhibit galleries, a reading room, and a small office for Cookie. The microfiche from the *Burpyville Gazette* was stored in a large walk-in closet off the reading room.

Cookie Bentley and Maddy Madison huddled in front of the reader, having loaded the spool of film for 1896. They had laid aside the microfiche for 1897, just in case. The Madison Meteorite had landed in November, the most common time of year for meteor showers. A meteor shower is the term used for a spike in the number of "shooting stars" that streak through the night sky.

Just to be sure, the two women started with the *Burpyville Gazette* for October and inched forward. Back then the newspaper was a weekly, making skimming easier.

Most of the news had to do with Burpyville. That town had been settled later than Caruthers Corners, but being closer to Indianapolis it had grown faster. There were squibs about city council meetings, petty crimes, visiting dignitaries, and occasional references to world news.

As it happened, 1896 was the year William McKinley had been elected president. Utah got admitted as the 45th state. Fanny Farmer wrote her first cookbook. The Dow

Jones Industrial Average was formed. Henry Ford built his first car, the Quadricycle. Ethiopia defended its independence from Italy, ending the First Italo-Ethiopian War. The Shanriku Earthquake killed more than 27,000 people in Japan. The first modern Olympic Games was held in Athens. And Sperry & Hutchinson began offering S&H Green Stamps.

The only mention of the Madison Meteorite was a short blurb on November 22:

Light in the Sky
CARUTHERS CORNERS — A bright light in the sky was reported last Friday. This comet was more luminescent than the planet Venus, which could be seen beside it in the evening sky. Some residents feared the world was coming to an end.

But nothing about the meteorite being recovered by a local farm boy. Or killing anybody.

~ ~ ~

The following year was more fruitful. In the microfiche for January 1897, Cookie and Maddy came across the following piece:

Falling Star Found
CARUTHERS CORNERS — A 14-year-old boy claims to have recovered a meteor that crashed to earth last November. Beauregard Madison has produced a rock slightly larger than a baseball that he says he recovered after seeing a light streaking through the early evening sky. It landed, he says, on his family's farm, giving him right of possession. Other than allowing friends to handle the blackened rock, he refused further comment about the rare astronomical occurrence. Neighbors say that the meteor knocked down a silo north of town. No other damage has been reported.

"They left the Third off his name," muttered Maddy as she read the short article. "Numbers have always been important in the Madison family."

"Oh, then why is there no Beauregard Madison V? You named your boys Bill and Fred."

Maddy offered a weak smile. "I've never been big on dynasties," she replied. "So I put my foot down. But Beau finally won the day. I agreed to name our third child after him."

"But that child turned out to be a girl – Tilly."

"A feminine form of Beauregard sounded stupid even to my heritage-minded hubby. So we named her after my mother's sister."

"Your adopted mother's sister," Cookie amended.

"I didn't know I was adopted back then," Maddy reminded her friend. "Katherine Taylor will always be the mother I knew. Sue Ann Polk never acknowledged me as her daughter."

"A shame."

"I only knew her as one of the crazy Polk sisters," sighed Maddy. "Imagine, passing her on the street and not knowing she was my mother."

They whirred through several more months of 1897 on the microfiche reader, but found no other references to the meteorite.

"Hmm," said Cookie Bentley. "We still need to see Beauregard Madison III's diary. Will you talk to your husband again?"

"I'll try. But he's awfully protective of it. I don't even know where he keeps it."

~ ~ ~

Mycroft Madison took up residence in the Madison

household, occupying Freddie's old room. N'yen had Bill's old room. Tilly's room had been turned into storage for Maddy's fabric scraps and sewing supplies.

Mikey showed no signs of moving out. Maddy, of course, was the perfect hostess. Beau huffed and puffed and scowled, even though he held his tongue.

Closest he came to speaking his mind was when he handed the *Burpyville Gazette* across the breakfast table to his brother, noting, "There's a Classified Section for rentals in the back pages. I know you'll be wanting to get your own place."

"No, I'm quite happy here," answered Mikey.

Later, Beau tried giving his brother a brochure for a local retirement village called Wabash Acres. "I hear you can buy these units for no money down."

"That's good because I have no money other than a pittance from Social Security. But I'm comfortable here with you."

"Yes, but –"

"I can't thank you and Maddy enough for taking me in, your poor destitute brother. After the way I left home in a huff, I'm surprised anyone would welcome me back to Caruthers Corners."

"What I'm trying to say is –"

"No, no, you don't have to say anything. Your generosity is duly noted. And much appreciated."

Double dog dang, thought Beau. *I'm never going to get rid of this freeloader*!

Chapter Eight

The Missing Diary

"Pooh Bear, I know you don't want to talk about your father finding that chunk of an asteroid, but Cookie's trying to trace down the folktale that someone got killed by it."

"Why not just leave that as conjecture?" Beau answered his wife. "Nothing to be gained by poking that particular snake with a stick."

"But why not clear up all the speculation?"

"Because no good can come of it. Family history is better served to drop the subject."

Maddy crossed her arms, looking stern. "It's a matter of clarifying facts about a historical event. And *you* know the truth. After all you have your father's diary."

"True."

"Where is that tattered old journal? I haven't seen it around the house in years."

"Oh, some place safe," he replied vaguely.

~ ~ ~

After retiring as president of Caruthers Corners Savings and Loan, Edgar Ridenour had devoted himself to outdoor pursuits, spending much of his time fishing on the Wabash River in his aluminum flat-bottom boat. He'd swapped his pin-stripped suits for cargo pants and baggy sweatshirts; let his thinning hair grow long; sported a bushy salt-and-pepper beard that made him look like a mountain man. But he still sat on the boards of the Savings and Loan, Burpyville Memorial, and a handful of other organizations, so occasionally he had to clean himself up and put on a good suit to attend a meeting. He hated this, but the terms of his retirement package at the bank required it.

His wife Lizzie didn't mind his transformation into a grizzled woodsman, for the couple had always lived separate lives in the same house, a cordial arrangement that comes with more than thirty years of dull marriage. Lizzie preferred a social life of parties and garden clubs and quilting bees. She had a knack for needlecrafts and had won the quiltmaking competition at the annual Watermelon Days festival several years in a row. Edgar was more of a misanthrope, inclined toward solitude and close friends.

While Edgar may have been the bank's president, Lizzie's grandfather had founded the institution. Lizzie came from money. It secretly irked her that with Maddy Madison's recent trust fund, her friend was now wealthier than she. Not that Lizzie had ever lorded her financial status over the other gals in the Quilters Club, but she'd enjoyed the self-image of being rich.

Edgar didn't mean to breach any confidentiality, but when his wife brought up the fact that Maddy couldn't find the diary written by Beau's father, he said, "Of course she can't. It's locked away in a safe deposit box at the Savings and Loan."

~ ~ ~

Bootsie dropped by the police station to bring her husband his Candesartan-Hydrochlorothiazid pills, a medication he took for high blood pressure. He'd forgotten his pillbox, a vintage Limoges that had belonged to his great aunt.

"Hi, Hon," Jim Purdue greeted her. "I appreciate the personalized delivery service."

"You'd lose your head if it wasn't attached," she chided. "Don't forget to take your medicine. Your blood pressure was 140/90 last time you visited Doc Habegger."

"Don't worry. That was just a bad day. I'm fine."

"You know hypertension runs in your family. Your cousin Bobby Ray has high blood pressure too."

The police chief grinned. "Yeah, but with his money he can afford to get massages, take yoga lessons, and vacation at Caribbean resorts where they serve piña coladas on the beach. Bobby Ray can chill out whenever or wherever he wants."

"Maybe we should vacation in the Caribbean this year."

"Hey, who died and left you a bag of money?"

Bootsie rolled her eyes. "Too bad I'm not a Hoople heir like Maddy ... or the granddaughter of a bank founder like Lizzie."

"Or the wife of a wealthy landowner like Cookie," added her husband. "Ben Bentley has more farm acreage than anybody in the county, except for maybe Boyd Aitkens."

"Too bad you married a poor girl. My daddy was a grocer. No trust fund for me."

"Yes, Melon Pickers Market was a great little store before Food Lion put him out of business. A shame."

"Broke his heart. He died shortly after that. I think he just gave up on life. Especially after my mom passed away."

"Too bad about your –"

The phone rang.

Jim Purdue picked it up. His dispatcher was out with a cold, one of those early spring sniffles. He suspected it was really allergies, some pollen that aggravated her sinuses. "Caruthers Corners Police Station," he barked. "Oh, hi Petie. Whatzup? Why you calling on the land line?"

There was a pause as he listened to Deputy Pete Hitzer, a scowl settling across his florid face. To Bootsie, the voice on the phone sounded like the buzzing of an angry wasp. Her husband kept saying, "Yeah ... yeah ...." And then hung up.

He grabbed his policeman's cap and pulled it snuggly onto his slick head. "Gotta go," he said to his wife. "A murder."

"W-who?" she asked.

"Beau Madison's brother Mycroft."

CHAPTER NINE

The Crime Scene

Pete Hitzer was working the crime scene when Chief Purdue showed up at Personally Yours Flowers & Gifts, the floral shop operated by Oliver Micherson and his partner Jeff Brown. According to Ollie, he'd discovered the body when he went out back to the refrigerated unit where they store flowers. Mycroft Madison had been sprawled on the floor.

Deputy Evers Gochnauer had been called in to help out. He was doing crowd control when the Chief arrived. Jim Purdue walked around back to inspect the crime scene. An old refrigerator truck was parked next to the shop, serving as a repository for an array of American Beauty roses, white carnations, enchantment lilies, gerbera daisies, pink wax flowers, liatris, tulips, button poms, snapdragons, golden aster, and hydrangeas. The door hung open, letting cool air escape.

Doc Medford was inside, bending over the body. Franklin D. Medford, MD, doubled as coroner. A general practitioner, his office was located next door to the Yost & Yost funeral home. That made things convenient.

"This is an easy one," he said to the police chief. "Head bashed in. Blunt force trauma."

"Murder weapon?"

The white-haired doctor stood and brushed off his

trousers. "Looks like it was this bag of rocks," he held them up with a latex-gloved hand. "The netting was swung like a sap."

"Rocks?"

"White river rocks – sometimes used in the bottom of vases to stabilize flowers. The floral shop both uses them and sells them by the bag. Five pounds for $15."

Chief Purdue bent over the corpse. "Looks like five pounds was enough to do the job. Back of his head's bashed in like a rotten melon."

"Somebody said this is Beau Madison's brother."

The Chief nodded. "Yep, no doubt about it. Except for the longish hair, he's the spittin' image of Beau."

~ ~ ~

"Mikey's dead?" Beauregard Madison could hardly comprehend this concept. He and his brother had been estranged for nearly thirty years, then barely kept in touch after they had reunited a dozen or so years back.

"Sorry, Beau," said Chief Jim Purdue, standing there on his friend's doorstep, cap in hand. Notifying next of kin was the hardest part of his job. "Hate to tell you, but looks like it was murder."

"Murder?" gasped Maddy, hands clutching her husband's arm. "Who would murder Mycroft? Nobody here even knows him."

"That's right, croaked Beau. "My brother only got in town last week. You know that, Jim. We had you and Bootsie over to celebrate the Prodigal Son's return."

"How did it happen? Was it a mugging?" asked Maddy.

"Dunno. Somebody ambushed him over at the flower shop – you know Ollie Micherson's place. Hit him on the back of his head, the dirty coward."

"Did Ollie or Jeff see it happen?" pressed Beau. His legs felt weak, but Maddy's hands gave him steady support.

"Ollie didn't have a clue till he went out back to get some roses for Roger and Doris Swartzendruber's thirtieth anniversary. That's when he found the ... uh ... your brother."

Maddy asked, "What was Mycroft doing over there? Buying flowers?"

"Nobody knows. He didn't come into the shop, according to Ollie."

"Maybe it was something else," reflected Beau. "You know about my brother."

Jim Purdue cleared his throat. "You're suggesting he was there because Ollie and Jeff are gay?"

Beau shrugged. "It's possible. Maybe he wanted to associate with people he had something in common with. Who else is there other than those two?"

"More than you might think," said the Chief. "People have secret lives."

~ ~ ~

Eggie Ettelman looked spiffy in his new double-breasted suit, sitting there in Bobby Ray Purdue's office. The town's second richest citizen maintained a small office in the Caruthers Corners Savings and Loan Building. The bank rented out space on its second floor.

"What can I do for the Treasury Department?" asked Bobby Ray. He looked confused by the man's unannounced appearance at his door this morning.

Eggie had flashed his phony credentials, a now-you-see-it now-you-don't slight of hand, after introducing himself as a US Treasury Agent. "We've found a slight discrepancy in your financial filings," he announced with pseudo authority.

"What filings?"

"That's just the problem. You didn't file the proper forms when you came into your new wealth."

"No, you have that wrong. I paid taxes on the money I got from selling those bank notes. You can talk to my accountant, if you like."

"Taxes are not the issue," asserted Eggie, trying to look very solemn.

"Then what's the problem?" Bobby Ray frowned. He looked ridiculous in his fringed leather sports jacket, beaded trousers, and crocodile-skin boots. It made him look like a 1940s singing cowboy. He even had a wide-brimmed Stetson on the coatrack behind him. His sartorial style had been wacky since becoming a multimillionaire.

"Well, those bank notes you found are like a treasure hunter finding a chest of doubloons on a sunken Spanish galleon. They belong to the government, not the finder."

"You're saying those Grand Watermelon notes didn't belong to me?"

"Exactly."

"But they belonged to my family. They were stored in a quilt made by my great-grandmother."

"Don't matter. Them Federal Reserve notes were like an unclaimed treasure. That makes them belong to the government, not you."

"Hold on there!" said Bobby Ray, standing up to demonstrate his alarm. "I'm going to call my lawyer.

You Feds aren't getting your grubby hands on my money."

"Now, now, calm down, Mr. Purdue. We don't plan to confiscate your funds. We merely want our cut."

"Your cut?"

"That's right. We have a procedure for settling issues like this out of court. According to our records you sold those notes for a sum slightly over $200,000,000. Our normal fee is 10% but in order to settle this matter swiftly and quietly, we will drop it to 5% – cash if you don't mind."

"That would be $10,000,000."

"A small pittance to put this issue to rest." Eggie smiled pleasantly. He could feel himself inches from becoming a very rich man. This dumb hick was falling for this hooey, no question about it.

"In cash? Isn't that unusual?"

"No, not at all. You just don't hear about these kinds of settlement because they're highly confidential."

"But getting that much cash together will be difficult. It'd fill a panel truck."

"No problem. We will provide an armored truck to pick up the money." Yeah, right. A Hertz rental van was more likely, thought Eggie.

"It could take days."

"Then you better get started. All you have to do is walk downstairs to the Savings and Loan and tell them you want to withdraw the money. Once we receive the $10-mil you'll be back in compliance with federal regulations."

Bobby Ray looked confused. "How come this didn't come up before?"

"Slipped through the cracks. Happens sometimes."

"Oh."

"Do we have a deal? Does Uncle Sam get his due?"

"Let me talk to the bank and get back to you."

~ ~ ~

Dr. Archimedes Claypool drove up from Bloomington for a meeting with the Caruthers Corners Historical Society. He wanted to go over his opening remarks for the Madison Meteorite exhibit with the executive director.

Having just heard about the murder of Beau's brother, Cookie Bentley was a bit distracted. Nonetheless, she showed the proper respect for such a distinguished astronomer. Archie Claypool was assistant director of the University of Indiana Bloomington's Kirkwood Observatory. And his textbook on meteors was considered a classic study of the celestial phenomenon.

Cookie's office was small, but not nearly as cluttered as her old digs in the building across town where the Historic Society had been housed before the Perricock Museum of Science & History opened its doors. The old location was scheduled to become a new quilting museum. The town owned a number of historic quiltworks that deserved a home – among them the Mad Matilda Wilkins Witch Quilt, the rare Reconciliation Quilt, the fake Beasley Heritage Quilt, and that tattered old quilt which once held those Grand Watermelon notes that had made Bobby Ray Purdue a wealthy man.

"I'm looking forward to the exhibit," said Dr. Claypool. "This is the first time the Madison Meteorite has ever been put on public view."

"We're very pleased to have the meteorite," Cookie

replied. "It has been in the Madison family since it was found by Beauregard Madison III in 1896."

"Would it be possible for me to see it in advance?"

"Why certainly. The meteorite is here in our storage room, awaiting its debut."

She led the pudgy astronomer through a door off her office, into a large windowless room that was stacked with boxes, old newspapers, filing cabinets, and an eclectic array of historical artifacts – ranging from a diorama of the Big Fire of 1899 to a 3-D model of the E Z Seat chair factory to a six-foot-tall wooden Indian in native costume.

"Forgive the clutter. We're still moving into this new space. We also recently inherited Col. Percival Perricock's various collectibles and still have that to sort through. They're stored on the third floor."

"Yes, I understand. Our own space debris collection is difficult to keep up with," said the astronomer. "NASA has been kind enough to loan us some moon rocks."

"Our space rock is over here," Cookie directed his attention to a table in the corner. Atop it on a folded blanket was the blackened meteorite. At first glance it looked like a charred bocce ball.

Dr. Claypool leaned forward to inspect it more closely. "Hmm, yes, you're right about that – this is definitely an aerolite."

"A what?"

"An aerolite is a stony meteorite, composed mainly of silicates. Essentially a rock. Aerolites account for about two-thirds of all meteorites."

"What are the other kinds?"

"Meteorites are traditionally divided into three broad categories: stony meteorites; metallic meteorites, largely composed of iron-nickel; and stony-iron meteorites that are a mixture of both metallic and rocky materials."

"So this is the most common kind of meteorite?"

"Yes, but even they are quite rare. In recorded scientific history, eye-witnessed falls have resulted only in about a thousand meteorite finds."

"Oh."

"Aside from the meteorite types I just described, cometary meteoroids form about 95% of *all* meteor showers that you see in the night sky."

"Cometary meteoroids?"

"Your common 'shooting star' that's seen in meteor showers."

"Are meteor showers dangerous?"

Dr. Claypool smiled. "Not really. While quite spectacular to watch, a meteor shower presents no real danger. You see, cometary meteoroids are usually composed of frozen methane, ammonia, water, carbon dioxide, carbon dust, and other trace materials. They vaporize high in the upper atmosphere and never reach earth."

"And the rock variety like ours?"

"Aerolite meteoroids rapidly lose mass due to ablation. Because of their high-speed collision with air molecules, the meteoroids' outer layer is continuously stripped away. Particles from dust size to a few kilograms mass are usually completely consumed in the atmosphere. So very few falls actually strike the earth."

"What's the biggest meteorite to ever strike earth?"

"Probably the asteroid that created the **Vredefort** Crater in South Africa. With an estimated radius of 118 miles, it is the world's largest known impact structure. That one occurred about two billion years ago."

"Was that the meteor that killed off the dinosaurs?"

"No, that one was thought to be the meteor that hit the Yucatán Peninsula 65 million years ago. It created the Chicxulub Crater, which has an estimated diameter of 106 to 186 miles. So Chicxulub might actually prove to be larger than Vredefort once more research is concluded."

"And that one did in the dinos?"

"Many scientists believe the six-mile-wide meteorite that hit the Yucatán Peninsula caused the extinction of the dinosaurs as well as killing off 75% of all plant and animal species on the earth. The date of this impact coincides precisely with the end of the Cretaceous Period."

"Six miles wide," she whistled. "That's big."

Dr. Claypool nodded. "Meteorites range in size from particles weighing only a few grams up to many miles wide. However, the largest known specimen we have is the Hoba West Meteorite, found in South Africa in 1920. It weighs 60 tons." He hefted the Madison Meteorite in his hand. "Yours weighs about ten pounds, I'd guess."

"Eleven pounds six ounces," Cookie said with pride.

"Will the Madison family be present at the

opening? Perhaps someone can say a few words about how it was found."

Cookie hesitated. "I expect the son will be here. But he's pretty tight-lipped about how the meteorite was found."

"A shame. We like to collect as much history of a find as we can."

"The Madisons are experiencing a tragedy. Beau Madison's brother was just found dead."

"Natural causes?"

"No, I'm afraid not. His head was bashed in."

"Murder ... or hit by a meteorite?"

Cookie didn't find the astronomer's joke very funny.

CHAPTER TEN

Cuckoo Crossing

Liz Ridenour took Aggie and N'yen along with her to interview Granny Crackleton. The Madison family was tied up at Yost & Yost with funeral arrangements. Getting the kids out of their hair was appreciated, even if no one knew Lizzie was taking them to Cuckoo Crossing.

Few locals would be comfortable going there.

Sarah Celine Crackleton – better known as Granny – had turned 97 last birthday, but she didn't look a day over 96. Her face was as wrinkled as a sun-dried apple. The old crone's birth occurred in a leap year: 1920, the same year that ushered in Prohibition, that women first voted in a national election in the US, and in which 180,000 died from an earthquake in China. Being born on February 29th of a bissextile year messes up the candles on the cake. Did that technically make her 24?

Granny Crackleton was the oldest resident of an area properly known as Crackleton Crossing, but town folks had dubbed it Cuckoo Crossing, a reference to rumors of inbreeding within the Crackleton family. The Crackletons were the predominant inhabitants of this little crossroads community just north of Never Ending Swamp.

Granny's son owned a general store at the crossroads, a way-stop that sold pop and cigarettes and watered-down gas. No locals ever stopped there, the store surviving from occasional patronage by unwary travelers. One of Granny's grandsons – an elfin man with six fingers on his right hand – ran the store. She lived on her own in a tumbledown house across the road from the store. Various relatives helped care for the elderly woman's needs.

Lizzie found Granny Crackleton rocking on her front porch. The old woman waved for the three visitors to join her. She was used to people who came from faraway to ask her about "the old days." Granny's colorful stories were legendary.

"I know who you are," the old woman pointed a knobby finger at Aggie. "The mayor's daughter. Am I right?"

"Yes, ma'am," Abby said politely. She had been raised to respect age.

"And who is this young Chinese boy?"

"Vietnamese," corrected N'yen. "I'm her cousin."

"Oh my. And people question the mix-n-match in my family."

"I'm adopted," he said. A simple statement of fact.

"We wondered if you could tell us about the meteorite that fell here in 1896," interjected Lizzie, her red hair flashing in the afternoon sun.

"Ha! 1896 was before my time."

"But I understand that years later you were told about it by the person who found it.

"You mean that falling star ol' Beauregard found in his daddy's pasture?"

"Yes, that one. Were there more?"

The old woman wrinkled her brow, squinting from one eye. "You see falling stars most ever' night. But few of 'em gets found."

"Beau Madison the Third found one."

"That he did. He showed it to me oncest. Looked like a shriveled up bowling ball."

"What did he say about finding it?" Lizzie pressed.

"Beauregard said he was out looking for a cow that had wandered off. It was late in the day, close to twilight. Said he heard a hissing sound and looked up to see this falling star shoot through the sky. It hit his daddy's silo with a bang. Hurrying over, he found that ol' comet buried in the ground nearby. So he fetched it home and showed it to his daddy. That was pretty much the end of it."

"What about the meteorite hitting somebody?" Aggie spoke up.

"Oh, you mean the boy in the silo," said Granny Crackleton. "That's a secret."

"A secret?" repeated Lizzie.

"Beauregard's daddy didn't want him to talk about it. Afraid they would be blamed for the boy gettin' hit by a falling star on their farm."

"Who was the boy?" asked N'yen.

"Ahh, that's the secret," Granny Crackleton said, refusing to say more.

~ ~ ~

Fatty Johnson announced at the Town Council Meeting that he planned to form The Ferdinand Aloysius Jinks Heritage Society as a means of honoring his ancestor. "Ferdinand Jinks deserves greater recognition for his role in founding this town," he summed up. "Ain't right that the Caruthers and Madisons get all the credit."

Mayor Mark Tidemore was chairing the council meeting as usual. Council members Edgar Ridenour,

Ben Bentley, and Police Chief Jim Purdue were present. Boyd Aitkens, also a council member, was on hand too. Beau Madison was absent due to the death in the family.

The audience was thin as usual. Most citizens were content to leave the business of running a small municipality to others. Hilda Hoople was there. So were Daniel Sokolowski and Big Bill Haney and Nell Grundy and Dr. Howard Carvel Oakman. Even Buddy Flynn and Big-Nose Evans and Fatty Johnson's idiot brother Clovis.

"We look forward to hearing more about your new organization," said the mayor, trying to move the agenda along. "I'm sure you will represent your great-grandfather's legacy well."

"Thank you," said Fatty. "I've hired a writer to do a book on Ferdinand Jinks, giving us the true account of the town's founding."

At that point Big-Nose Evans stood up. "You're just sore the town didn't get named after ol' Ferdie Jinks," he said, pointing a finger at Fatty Johnson. "What a stupid name Jinksville woulda been."

Fatty struggled to his feet, red in the face. "And you're just sticking up for your own self-aggrandizing relatives. Everybody knows you're a Caruthers on your mother's side."

"So what?" retorted Big-Nose, not a very articulate fellow. "You can't change history, Fatty Johnson."

"Hey, you can't talk that way to my brother!" shouted Clovis Johnson, shaking a fist in Big-Nose's direction. Pudgy and white bearded, he looked like a shorter version of his sibling.

"Let's see you stop me, you dummy."

"I'll –"

Klak! Klak!

Mark the Shark rapped his gavel to bring order to the meeting. "That's enough, boys. This is not a kindergarten playground."

~ ~ ~

Bootsie Purdue never heard a conspiracy theory she didn't halfway believe. So it caught her attention when Maisie Walters said, "Lucky the murderer didn't bludgeon Beau by mistake. He and his brother look so much alike."

Bootsie had been having a slice of watermelon pie at the Cozy Café. A secret vice that affected her weight, she was now about 40 pounds over her doctor's recommendation. Maisie used to be the head waitress until she came into a bundle of money and bought the place. Turns out, she and Maddy were twin sisters, joint heirs to the Hoople Quadruplets fortune.

"What did you just say?" Bootsie looked up, almost spilling her coffee.

"That Beau and his brother looked a lot alike. Both tall drinks of water. Strong profiles that oughta be on a coin. Similar walks and gestures. They looked more like twins than me and Maddy do."

"Oh my. You don't suppose Beau was the intended victim, do you?"

"Who's to say?"

"I've gotta go tell my husband."

Maisie could tell the police chief's wife was upset. She didn't finish her pie.

Chapter Eleven

Watermelon and Cucumber Sandwiches

Maddy Madison saw Fatty Johnson and his brother walking out of the Town Hall. They looked angry, like cats that had fallen into a rain barrel.

She was on her way to her daughter's house across from the town square. Tilly and her husband Mark lived in the old Taylor House, where Maddy had grown up. She paused on the sidewalk as Fatty and Clovis passed, nodding her hello. They harrumphed a reply, but kept on walking. Rude, as usual.

As they resumed their conversation, she heard the words, "... forget about the meteorite. That was a long time ago."

Hmm, what was that about?

She watched the two men waddle down the street, Fatty and his look-alike brother. Two peas in a pod, she thought. Grumpy, ill-tempered men.

Just then she sighted Ben Bentley and Edgar Ridenour coming out of the big brick building. She waved at them, and they beelined toward where she stood at the edge of the square.

"Hi Maddy. How are you and Beau holding up?" said the farmer. Cookie's husband was short and stout, like one of those warrior dwarves in *Lord of the Rings*.

"As well as can be expected. Beau is upset, but it's not like he and his brother had been close for the past forty years."

"Anything we can do?" asked Lizzie's husband. The former banker looked quite rustic, hair shaggy and face hidden behind a bramble-bush beard. But he was wearing a suit today.

"Beau may need some company over the next few days. Perhaps you and N'yen could take him fishing between now and the funeral. You might just catch Big Calvin, the elusive catfish."

"Yes, a good idea. Ben, you want to join us?"

"Sorry, but I have duties with the Haney Bros. petting zoo. But I'll pay Beau a visit after your fishing excursion. I'm sure you and Beau will have some lies to tell about the one that got away."

"Will do. See you later, Maddy."

She caught Edgar Ridenour's arm. "One more thing. Lizzie said you told her that my hubby keeps his father's diary in a safe deposit box at the bank. Is that true?"

Edgar shrugged. "I guess it's all right to tell you, Maddy – you being the wife and all. He's kept it there for some years now. I don't think he's ever been back to the box since depositing that dusty old journal in it."

"Thanks," she smiled. Patting him on the arm reassuringly. "Now that I know where it is, I just have to find a way of getting inside. Cookie needs to read it prior to the Madison Meteorite exhibit."

"That's week after next, isn't it?" said Ben. "I know she's been trying to find out more about that old rock's history. But I doubt Beau gonna come around so quickly."

"That's right," nodded Edgar. "He's never been keen on talking about the diary's contents. And now with his brother's death –"

"Guess I've got my work cut out," sighed Maddy, turning and continuing down the sidewalk toward the Taylor house.

~ ~ ~

Tilly fixed a pitcher of watermelon tea. She and her mother settled in the parlor and sipped at their tea while nibbling on tiny watermelon and cucumber sandwiches. Maddy was famished, having missed lunch while at the funeral home with Beau.

Turns out, there would be no actual funeral here. Mycroft's sons were having the body shipped back to New York where he would be interred in Woodlawn Cemetery. He'd lived in the Big Apple for over thirty years and that's where Mycroft Jr. and Matthew wanted him buried, close to them.

Early on, when trying to deny his sexual orientation, Mycroft had married and sired two children. Mycroft Jr. was a successful accountant in Manhattan; married with two kids. Matthew was a theater manager in New Haven, Connecticut, having followed in his father's footsteps; the jury was out on his sexuality. But they were Mycroft's family more than the relatives he'd left behind in Indiana some forty years ago.

"Is Dad very sad about losing his only brother?" asked Tilly. She passed the plate of tiny sandwiches to her mother for a second helping.

"More confused, I think. He hardly knew his brother. Mikey left home so long ago. And I think he's trying to come to terms with the LGBTQ thing. Your dad is more homophobic than he'd like to admit."

"And you?"

"To each his own, I say."

Tilly nodded. "I always thought it was cool having a gay uncle. Didn't he once win a Tony for directing a play on Broadway?"

"Nominated. But still that's a great honor."

"Do you think his death had anything to do with him being gay? After all, he was killed at Personally Yours Flowers & Gifts. And Ollie and Jeff don't make a secret of their orientation."

"I doubt it. Cookie's former brother-in-law is gentle as a lamb. And Ollie doesn't have a mean bone in his body. He went to school with me and Beau and Mycroft."

"So that's what Uncle Mikey was doing there at Personally Yours – catching up with an old school chum?"

"That or buying flowers. After all, Valentine's Day is this coming Tuesday."

~ ~ ~

Bootsie Purdue caught up with Maddy at Tilly's house. She was pleased to find several watermelon and cucumber sandwiches left over. She hadn't finished her pie at Cozy Café.

"Your sister Maisie put me onto it," said the police chief's wife. "The murderer may have been targeting Beau instead of his brother. After all, they look alike. And hardly anybody knew Mycroft had come back to Caruthers Corners."

"Oh, that's silly," Maddy waved away her friend's cockamamie theory. "Beau has lived here all his life. If someone wanted to murder him, there's been plenty of opportunity before now."

"Aunt Bootsie, you *do* get wrapped up in your conspiracy theories," chided Tilly. "Remember when you got the idea that microwaves cause cancer?"

"They do! I won't have a microwave oven in my house."

"Without a microwave oven how will Kellyann Conway send you secret messages?" teased Maddy.

"Scoff if you like, but Jim and I both voted for Donald Trump."

"*Tsk, tsk*," said Maddy. "Don't forget the Quilters Club rule: no politics discussed among friends."

"Speaking of the Quilters Club," said Tilly, "are you girls going to find Uncle Mikey's murderer? After all, you consider yourselves amateur detectives."

Maddy sighed. "We can't even figure out who was killed by a fireball in 1896. What chance do we have of finding a clever murderer?"

CHAPTER TWELVE

The Radio-Controlled Robot

"Stand back!" warned N'yen as he pressed the red button on his controller. His cousin Aggie moved a few steps behind him as Ralph the Radio-Controlled Robot lumbered forward, a three-foot-tall mechanical man reminiscent of the robot on that *Lost in Space* TV program. It moved on tracks, like a small tank. The arms went up and down, waving metal claws instead of hands.

Aggie's dog barked at it.

"It works!" squealed Aggie, a grin parsing her face.

"Of course it does," replied N'yen. "I rewired it myself. This robot's twice as good as the out-of-the-box version."

"Let's see it pick something up," demanded the girl, clapping her hands. She might be an early teen in years, but at heart she was still a kid.

"No biggie," replied her cousin. Then with a buzzing sound the robot rolled forward, stopped in front of a screwdriver that had been left on the floor, bent forward slightly and gasped it with the pneumatic claws.

"Wow."

"Easy as pie," said N'yen. "Speaking of which, I wonder if there's any watermelon pie left."

"Let's go see."

"Sounds like a plan."

~ ~ ~

Bobby Ray Purdue showed up at the police station.

The Chief had just returned from the Town Council Meeting. "Hey, cuz, got a favor to ask," the young millionaire greeted the policeman.

"What favor's that?" asked Jim Purdue warily. Last time Bobby Ray asked for a favor, Jim had received a reprimand for complying. Beau had been mayor then, essentially his boss. The town's police force did not provide private security, Beau had chastised him.

Now here was his cousin again. "Can you check a guy out for me?"

"Bobby Ray, that's not a service we normally supply."

"I know, I know. But I need your help, cuz."

"Who's this guy you want me to run a check on," asked Chief Purdue. Still not convinced.

"Calls himself Elbert Ettelman. Says he's a Treasury Agent, but I think something might be hinky about him."

"Why so?

"Claims I owe the government money. But he wants the payment in cash."

The police chief pushed his cap back to rub his smooth head. "That doesn't sound right. How much money?"

"Ten mil."

Jim Purdue whistled. "That's quite a sum. I hope you haven't given him anything. Doesn't smell right to me."

"So you'll look into it?"

"Sit tight, Bobby Ray. I'll make some calls. Get back to you tomorrow."

~ ~ ~

Ollie Micherson told a reporter from the *Burpyville Gazette* that he was convinced Mycroft Madison's death had been a hate crime. "The fact that he was killed at my place of business was meant to send a signal that gays are not welcome in this community."

Mayor Mark Tidemore issued a rebuttal. "Caruthers Corners is a friendly town," he said for the record. "Mr. Micherson has been a successful businessman here for more than twenty years. Two years ago, he was chosen as the Chamber of Commerce's Man of the Year. That certainly demonstrates his acceptance hereabouts."

Ken Wurgler, head of the Chamber of Commerce, confirmed that sentiment to the *Burpyville Gazette*. "Oliver Micherson and his partner Jeff Brown add to our cultural richness," he said. "They are considered two of our leading citizens."

"No, we're not investigating this as a hate crime," Police Chief Jim Purdue was quoted in the article. "We think Mycroft Harrington Madison was simply in the wrong place at the wrong time. He likely interrupted a burglary and was murdered by the intruder."

Nonetheless, the headline proclaimed:

Hate Crimes Erupt in Indiana
Gay Community Lives in Fear

This was the kind of sensationalism that had found its way onto the front page after the acquisition of the *Burpyville Gazette* by the Nightley Newspapers Group. Josiah Nightley's papers and tabloids often carried reports of Elvis sightings and UFOs. It sold papers.

~ ~ ~

On Friday a small memorial service was held for Mycroft Madison. The turnout amounted to Beau and Maddy's family and a few close friends, being that Mikey was a relative newcomer to the Caruthers Corners scene.

Police Chief Jim Purdue had released the body and Yost & Yost had shipped it back to New York per the request of Mycroft's sons. The death remained an Open Homicide on the books. There were no new clues.

After the awkward eulogy by Rev. Copeland (he'd never met Mikey Madison), Maddy's gal pals surrounded her on the church steps. "Don't worry, we're going to solve this one," Bootsie assured her.

"Jim will kill you if you stick your nose in this investigation," cautioned Maddy. "This is murder – not stolen dinosaur bones or runaway circus boys."

"Never you mind my hubby," Bootsie assured her. "He understands this is family."

"That's exactly right," nodded Lizzie. "You're our sister. Or as close to it as anyone can come." Fact is, none of the Quilters Club women had any siblings – other than Maddy with her newfound twin.

"One for all and all for *et cetera*," declared Cookie, placing her hand on Maddy's.

"Yes," said Maddy's granddaughter Aggie. "The Quilters Club is on the case. Nobody can kill my great uncle and get away with it."

Chapter Thirteen

Four Alarm Fire

Fire Chief Freddie Madison got the call – a house fire on Melon Rind Road. That had to be Bobby Ray Purdue's big showplace, the only structure on that private stretch of roadway.

"Everybody to the truck," he called to the crew on duty. As usual, Freddie was first to slide down the pole.

As he raced toward the pumper truck, his fire hat slipped from his hand and tumbled under the big red vehicle. "Drat!" he cursed, stooping to retrieve it. That's when he spotted the pressure cooker sitting on the concrete floor directly under the truck.

"Whoa!" he said. "What's this?"

Then it came to him like a flash – a bomb.

Those Boston Marathon bombers had used pressure cookers with timers to cause mass destruction that tragic day in April 2013. There could be no other explanation for the squat silver pot being beneath the truck.

He stood up, frantically motioning for everybody to get out of the station. "Bomb!" he shouted. "Evacuate, evacuate!"

Outside on the sloping driveway, Freddie got his bearings. "Willy, you boys take the old pumper on the call. It's parked behind the Town Hall. Donnie, phone Chief Purdue. Roy, keep everybody away from the firehouse. No telling how much damage that bomb might do sitting there under No. 12's gas tank."

It was more excitement than when the old shoe factory had burned down.

~ ~ ~

Mayor Tidemore squatted down to peer underneath the fire truck from what he hoped was a safe distance. "What's supposed to set it off?"

"Hard to tell with a homemade bomb," said Chief Purdue. "Might be hooked to a timer. Or rigged to go off when you start the truck. Or waiting for a phone call."

"Sometimes homemade devices go off on their own," offered Ben Bentley. "A jiggle can do it." He'd served briefly in Desert Storm and knew something about IED's. "Depends on the skill of the bombmaker."

"Is this a terrorist attack?" asked Beau Madison. He'd been called in by his son-in-law. Beau had dealt with a few M14 anti-personnel mines in Vietnam, the ones called toe poppers.

"Not likely," replied Edgar Ridenour. He'd come along with Beau for the ride. "Caruthers Corners can't be very high on the ISIS target list."

Antiques dealer Daniel Sokolowski spoke up. "What about one of those homegrown terrorists? What do they call them – Lone Wolves? They get radicalized over Facebook, I hear."

"This is all Bill Gates' fault," grumbled Boyd Aitkens. "If he hadn't invented the Internet ..."

"Bill Gates didn't invent the Internet," N'yen spoke up. The boy had come down to the Fire Station with his grandfather.

"That's right," Boyd Aitkens corrected himself. "It was Al Gore."

"No," said N'yen. "A bunch of people were involved. But Vincent Cerf and Robert Kahn are considered the fathers of the Internet because they invented the TCP/IP protocol that made the Internet possible."

"The what —?"

The boy said patiently, "Transmission Control Protocol or Internet Protocol, that's the basic communication language of the Internet."

"Sure, I knew that," said the watermelon farmer.

"What do we do about this bomb?" the mayor asked Freddie Madison. "We leave it there, it will blow up the whole firehouse."

"All I can think of is to call in the bomb squad from Indianapolis. They have a robot that can remove this explosive device."

"I have a robot," said N'yen.

Chapter Fourteen

The Mechanical Man Goes Into Action

"Everybody stand back," ordered Chief Purdue. "This thing could blow."

The crowd backed up.

"How far?" somebody asked.

"Dunno," said the fire chief. "I'd err on safety. Why don't you folks move over to the edge of the town square."

Beau Madison said, "N'yen, you should stand back too. Can't you operate your robot from over there?"

"Don't think so. I'm not sure the signal will reach that far. Besides, from over there I can't see to maneuver my robot under the fire truck. I have to get hold of that bomb."

Freddie said, "Maybe we can shield him with something. How about Darnell Watson's snowplow?"

"That's a good idea," said Mayor Tidemore. "Let me call Darnell and see how fast we can get that plow down here."

Twenty minutes later Darnell Watson pulled up in his big green John Deere SP10 tractor. "Here you go," he called down to the mayor. "If this baby gets damaged the town's gonna buy me a new one. I'm just a contractor. This is my personal equipment, not town property."

"Yeah, yeah. Park it right over there," Mark Tidemore pointed.

"Okay."

"Darnell, you got any goggles in there?" asked Beau. "If so, give them to my grandson."

"Here you go. Got a hard hat too, you want that."

"Hand them down," said Freddie, reaching up for them.

The twelve-year-old boy squatted behind the oversized snowplow blade, wrapped in Pete Hitzer's bulletproof vest, with thick goggles covering his eyes, and a hard hat capping his head like an inverted soup bowl. Ralph the Radio-Controlled Robot stood in front of the sturdy metal blade, looking like a three-foot-tall espresso machine about to gurgle out its first cup.

"You sure your robot can lift that pressure cooker? Looks heavy to me," observed Edgar Ridenour.

"Doubt it can lift it, Uncle Edgar. But it might be able to drag it out into the open."

The police chief said, "If we get it out of the station, down in that field over there, we can explode it safely."

"I'll try, Uncle Jim.

"That little tin robot looks pretty flimsy for such a large task," said Boyd Aitkens.

"Yes, it's really just a toy," agreed Ben Bentley, the two farmers seemingly in agreement. "He bought it at the Dollar Store."

"A bucket of bolts," nodded Deputy Hitzer.

"I made a few alterations," responded N'yen defensively. "Doubled the memory, reprogrammed the movements, reinforced the tensile strength of the arms, increased its traction. Ralph is souped up."

"Ralph –?"

"That's his name. Said so on the box."

Chief Purdue interrupted. "Let's get this going. Sooner we drag that pressure cooker out of there and explode it, the better."

"Be careful," cautioned Beau. "That thing may go off on its own." In Vietnam he'd seen MD-82s go off with little provocation. Activation pressure was only 4 to 5 kg. Who knew what to expect with a homemade bomb?

"Okay, Ralph, do your stuff," N'yen said to his robot as he pressed the activation button. There was a buzzing sound and the "bucket of bolts" moved forward with a lurch.

~ ~ ~

First problem came when Ralph reached the fire truck: The robot was too tall to go under it. How was it to retrieve the bomb if it couldn't get to it?

"Add air to the truck's tires," suggested Deputy Evers Gochnauer. "That'll raise the frame."

"Put a jack under the truck," proposed Buddy Flynn. He ran the Texaco station out on Highway 21. "Want me to go get a couple of hydraulic jacks?"

After much debate, it was decided that disturbing the truck might set off the bomb. "Much too dangerous," concluded Chief Purdue.

"I'll fix it," said N'yen, directing his mechanical man to return to the safety of the snowplow. "Gimme a screwdriver. A medium-sized flathead."

"I'll get one from my truck," volunteered Buddy Flynn. He went dashing down the street toward the Town Hall parking lot where he'd left his AAA tow truck.

"The solution," explained the Vietnamese boy as he

tinkered on Ralph, "is simple. If you can't raise the truck, lower the robot." He removed the "head" from the mechanical device. "Only thing in here's a tiny camera. Without it, I'll have to work by my own eyesight. Fortunately, I've got 20/20 vision."

Now a foot shorter, the automated robot rolled beneath the fire truck with an inch to spare. It stopped just short of the pressure cooker, careful not to touch it. "Here's the tricky part," said the boy. He fiddled with the dials on his controller and the robot raised an arm, the claw open. "I'm going to try to hook onto one of the cooker's handles."

A buzzing sound could be heard from under the truck. N'yen was lying on his belly in order to see the robot as it reached out for the bomb. *Clink*, the claw closed on the plastic handle with the finality of a cop slapping handcuffs on a burglar. "Got it," he said.

"Now drag it out," instructed Chief Purdue.

The buzzing sound increased. The rubber tracks spun on the cement floor of the firehouse. The pressure cooker moved a few inches. Nothing exploded.

"Keep 'er coming," urged the police chief.

"You got it moving," encouraged the fire chief.

"Careful," said the boy's grandfather.

"It's working," admitted Boyd Aitkens.

Boom! went the explosion.

CHAPTER FIFTEEN

The Dust Clears

The explosion was smaller than expected. Amateur bombmaking to blame. But it did destroy the Caruthers Corners Fire Department's pumper truck No. 12. The bomb would have killed or seriously injured anyone in the driver's seat. Fortunately, the firehouse itself wasn't damaged, the truck blanketing the blast. The cement floor was cracked, but that was easy enough to repair.

N'yen and the men crouching behind the blade of the John Deere snowplow were safe. Darnell Watson inspected his vehicle but could find no damage.

"There goes my new fire truck," groaned Freddie Madison. "Only had it a few weeks."

"Better it than you," said Police Chief Jim Purdue, putting a reassuring hand on the fire chief's shoulder. "If you hadn't spotted that pressure cooker under the truck, no telling what tragedy might've happened."

"I dropped my hat —"

"Don't worry about the truck," counseled his dad. "Your mother's trust fund will buy the town another one. Right, Mark?"

Mark the Shark nodded. "I'm sure it will," he confirmed. In addition to being the town's mayor and married to Beau and Maddy's daughter, he also served as executive director for the small foundation his mother-in-law had set up to manage her inheritance from the Hoople Quadruplets Foundation.

"What about Ralph?" said the Vietnamese boy.

"Who?"

"My robot. He got blown to kingdom come."

"Died in the line of duty," said Chief Purdue. "The police department will buy you another one out of its discretionary funds."

"But the Dollar Store only had one, a leftover from Christmas."

"Something else you might want?"

N'yen thought for a moment, his face squinched up like a squirrel contemplating a juicy acorn. He thought about the Madison Meteorite. The exhibit was opening at the Historical Society week after next. "I know," he said in a flash of inspiration. "I want a telescope."

~ ~ ~

"What was that all about?" the mayor asked the men standing around the demolished fire truck. The No. 12 lettering on the truck's side appeared sooty and scorched. The red metal jagged and bent from the bomb.

"Beats me," said Freddie. "Who would have a grudge against the fire department? We keep houses from burning down."

"Speaking of which, we just got back from Bobby Ray's house on Melon Rind Road. A false alarm," reported Willy Sutton. The fireman claimed to be a direct descendant of the famous bank robber, but nobody believed him.

"Obviously a ruse to get you boys down to the truck," said the police chief.

"This looks like it might've been a new pressure cooker," said Deputy Pete Hitzer, examining the scraps of metal under the truck. Everything was wet and sodden, the bomb having ruptured the pumper's water tank. At least any threat of fire had been avoided by the sudden deluge.

"Where would somebody buy a pressure cooker?" asked Mark, turning to his father-in-law. Beau Madison used to manage the Ace Hardware here in town, before Home Depot came in with its big selection and low prices.

"That's easy. Either Home Depot, Wal-Mart down in Burpyville, someplace in Indy, or from Amazon."

"We can check out Home Depot and Wal-Mart," said Deputy Gochnauer. "But Amazon's impossible ... and finding a place in Indianapolis would be like looking for a needle in a haystack."

Chief Purdue nodded. "Okay, Petie, you take Home Depot. Evers, you get Wal-Mart. And don't dawdle."

"Do we know of anybody local who knows how to make a bomb?" asked Mayor Tidemore.

"I know how to make a bomb," said N'yen.

"Besides Mr. Science here?"

"The M14s and Claymores I saw in Vietnam were mass produced. Never got near enough to figure out how they worked," said Beau.

"The improvised explosive devices I saw in Iraq were made by the other side, not us," said Ben Bentley. "But any kid –" he nodded toward N'yen "– can get instruction on how to build a bomb off the Internet."

"I blame Bill Gates," Boyd Aitkens repeated.

"That's how the Boston bombers learned," Edgar Ridenour pointed out. He watched a lot of Fox News when not fishing.

"Hey, I didn't do it," protested N'yen.

"Don't worry, son," said the police chief. "Nobody suspects you. Remember, I'm going to buy you a telescope to thank you for your help."

"Wasn't much help," the boy groused. "That bomb blew up my robot."

"Was the bomb on a timer?" asked the mayor.

"Not likely. The perp couldn't be sure when the firemen would be in the truck," said the police chief.

"Sure, they could," argued Willy Sutton. "He phoned in a false alarm."

"But the truck would have been long gone by the time it blew up, if I hadn't spotted it," Freddie pointed out.

"A telephone signal?" the mayor tried a different scenario.

Chief Purdue shook his head. "No, if the perp had that kinda control of the timing, he could've blown it up when Freddie bent down to retrieve his hat."

"Motion sensitive most likely," said the boy. "Probably had a wire hooked to the undercarriage, so it would go off when the truck drove out."

"And that's why it went off when N'yen tried to drag it out," Beau nodded. Made sense.

"But who would have a grudge against the fire department?" Freddie posed the question.

"Or the town," added Mark Tidemore.

"Or maybe Freddie," piped up Willy Sutton. "He would've been driving the truck."

"Me?"

"Well, somebody did kill your uncle last week," shrugged Willy. "Maybe the grudge is against the entire Madison family."

CHAPTER SIXTEEN

More Threats

"Three mysteries to solve," counted Agnes Tidemore. The Quilters Club had gathered as usual on Tuesday afternoon at the Senior Recreational Center. They were finishing up the Community Quilt for Willamina Haney. The woman was lingering, so they sewed as fast as they could.

"Three?" said Lizzie, confused.

"The meteorite mystery, the murder of Uncle Mikey, and now the bombing at the firehouse," Aggie ticked them off.

"Maybe only two, if Willy Sutton's right," said Bootsie. Looking for a conspiracy.

"A vendetta against the Madisons?" scoffed Maddy. "Don't be silly."

That was before the threat to Freddie's brother Bill.

~ ~ ~

"I'm okay," Bill Madison assured his mom on the phone that night. "The car's totaled, but I walked away without a scratch. Let's hear it for the Subaru's three-ring steel-frame construction. Otherwise I would've been squashed like a bug."

"Oh my," said Maddy.

"What happened?" demanded Beau, picking up the extension in the den. Maddy was on the kitchen line.

"Police say somebody cut my break lines. I hit a brick wall – literally. Fortunately, I had my seatbelt on."

"Cut your brake lines?" repeated Beau.

"You don't think Kathy would hire somebody to do me in, do you?" Bill and his wife had been going through an acrimonious divorce. That's why N'yen was living with his grandparents.

"Surely not," Maddy spoke up. "She wouldn't try to *kill* you."

"Well, somebody did," said her son, his voice sounding far away over the phone line.

~ ~ ~

"Better watch your step," said Jim Purdue when Beau brought up the idea of somebody being out to get the Madisons. First Mycroft, then Freddie, now Bill.

"Doesn't make sense. We don't have any enemies. At least none angry enough to try to kill the whole family."

"No one has made an attempt on *your* life yet," the police chief pointed out. "But if that theory's correct, you'd likely be next on the list."

"Maybe the killer got Mikey by mistake. Took him to be me."

The chief nodded. "That's Bootsie's theory."

"What about Tilly. Both her brothers have been targeted. Is she in any danger?"

"I'll have a word with Mark the Shark. He'll watch out for her and Aggie. You keep an eye on Maddy and N'yen."

"So you think there's a real threat?"

"I think we better not take any chances."

CHAPTER SEVENTEEN

Another Assassination Attempt

Maddy and Beau spent Valentine's at home, skipping the annual dance at the Town Hall. Tilly and Mark went, him being the mayor and all, but they sent Aggie to spend the evening with her Grammy and Grampy and cousin N'yen.

Safety first, Maddy had agreed. She and Beau were taking the threat seriously.

Aggie was bummed, for she'd been expecting to see Bobby Elwood at the dance. She had kind of a crush on him. She'd just started wearing lipstick.

Her cousin N'yen told her that makeup was a primitive custom invented by the Ancient Sumerians about 5,000 years ago. "Egyptian Pharaohs used makeup too. They wore lipstick to denote social status, not gender," he pointed out. "Cleopatra used crushed bugs to create a red color for her lips."

"Yuck," said Aggie.

"Don't worry. Your lipstick doesn't contain any bugs. It's a combination of pigments, oils, wax, and emollients. However, the FDA has found lead in most popular brands. Even low levels of lead affect IQ, attention span, and academic achievement. Since lead accumulates in the body, the effects of lead exposure are not able to be corrected."

"Oh my, am I going to be mentally impaired?"

"Probably no more than you already are," jibed her cousin.

"What makes you think I'm mentally impaired, Mr. Smarty Pants?"

"Because you put that gloop on your lips. Ergo, you must be stupid."

"What about other makeup? I want to use eyeliner but Mom won't let me. Says I have to wait till I'm sixteen."

"Queen Victoria declared that all makeup was improper, vulgar, and acceptable only for use by actors."

"I might become an actor when I grow up," mused Aggie. "It would be fun to be a movie star."

"If you became a movie star, could you get me tickets to your movies?"

"Of course, silly. You could be president of my fan club."

"Here," said N'yen. "I got you a Valentine card." He thrust the squarish envelope toward her.

"I've got you one too!" They exchanged cards.

Aggie's Valentine to N'yen read: **YOU STOLE MY HEART. GIVE IT BACK OR I'LL CALL THE POLICE!**

His card to her announced: **BE MY VALENTINE. NOBODY ELSE WOULD HAVE YOU.**

She'd also bought a Valentine card for Bobby Elwood, but that would have to wait.

~ ~ ~

There was a bit of excitement at the Valentine's dance. Someone took a shot at Mark Tidemore ... or maybe it was at his wife. The bullet gouged into a wooden column, the hole equidistant between the pair, so it was hard to tell which one had been the target.

Police Chief Purdue thought the shooter had been

in the town square across the street, maybe hiding behind the big oak tree at the corner. He figured the shot came from a semiautomatic pistol, judging by the 9mm slug found in the column, but that was a heckuva shot with a handgun. Lucky to hit the building at that distance.

Deputy Hitzer thought it was probably some drunk showing off with a loaded pistol. But given the attacks on the Madison family, Chief Purdue pegged it as another attempt by the killer of Beau's brother. He had Petie Hitzer and the three part-time deputies fan out around the town square, looking for somebody with a gun, but after a half-hour search they gave up. The perp had vanished as smoothly as Mandrake the Magician. Only thing missing was a puff of smoke.

CHAPTER EIGHTEEN

The Shooting Star Quilt

Despite Beau's strenuous objection, Maddy chose to drive down to Indianapolis with her Quilters Club pals on Thursday morning. They were taking Aggie and N'yen along as "junior members," although Aggie would have objected to that diminutive description.

They foursome had decided to go see the so-called *Shooting Star Quilt* that had been sewn by Mary Louise Madison, Beau's grandmother. It was on display at the Indiana State Museum. The kids went along for the ride, with the promise that N'yen could pick out a telescope to replace his destroyed robot. Chief Purdue – "Uncle Jim" to N'yen – had given the boy a crisp, new $100 bill.

Thus their first stop was at Fry Electronics in Fishers, a suburb of Indianapolis. N'yen selected a Celestron AstroMaster 114EQ telescope with a pre-assembled tripod. It cost more than $100 (even on sale) but Maddy contributed the extra $60 on the condition he not tell his Grampy. And to even-up the gifting, she bought Aggie a Nikon S3500 20.1 Megapixel Camera with a selfie stick. It was fun being rich.

Part of the spending spree could be attributed to Maddy's nerves being on edge, quite understandable with her losing a brother-in-law and coming close to losing her two sons and daughter within a week's time.

Beau was sticking close to home, not taking any chances. But Maddy felt perfectly safe with her ya-ya girlfriends surrounding her like Secret Service bodyguards.

Still …

"Do you really think someone is targeting my family?" she asked while the kids were busy picking out their presents.

"No doubt about it," replied Bootsie. "I bet an actuary would say the odds are a zillion-to-one against four members of the same family being attacked only days apart."

"Gee, I don't know about that," said Maddy. She wouldn't recognize an actuarial table if she saw one.

"Coincidences aren't just random happenings," insisted Bootsie. "Don't you think there's a connection between the deaths of John F. Kennedy, Robert Kennedy, and Martin Luther King?"

"I'm not so sure about Martin Luther King being part of that," interjected Cookie.

"Right," nodded Lizzie. "Dr. King was a different conspiracy entirely." She read the *National Inquirer* to keep up on such things.

"You think there's a conspiracy to get the Madison family?" Maddy's voice quivered.

"Absolutely," said Bootsie. "But don't you worry. The Quilters Club is going to unmask the culprit."

"Unmask what culprit?" asked Aggie, walking up just then. She carried her new camera and selfie stick over her shoulder like a sergeant at arms.

"The mad dog killer who's trying to wipe out your entire family," declared Bootsie, carried away with her dire theory.

"*Eek*! I'm gonna die?"

"Don't be afraid," said N'yen, joining the conversation. He carried his new telescope in his arms like a prized trophy. "Didn't you just hear Aunt Bootsie? The Quilters Club is going to catch the killer."

~ ~ ~

Founded in 1863 during the Civil War, the Indiana State Museum has moved locations several times over the years – from the State Capital Building to the old City Hall to its current facilities adjacent to the Indiana Central Canal. It has been there on the grounds of the White River State Park since 2001. The museum contains exhibits ranging from prehistoric mastodons to contemporary art. It also houses the largest IMAX screen in the entire state.

Aggie used her selfie stick to make a snapshot of her and N'yen in front of the angled glass façade. Then she left her camera in the car because photography was not allowed inside the museum. N'yen, however, refused to relinquish his new telescope, carrying the 17-pound instrument in his arms like a baby.

The group was there to see the famous *Shooting Star Quilt*. The 85" x 108" counterpane was displayed on a high wall in a second-floor gallery devoted to Hoosier handicrafts. Craning their necks, they looked up at the depiction of the meteorite that struck the Madison farm at the turn of the last century.

"Look, there's Beau's father, Beauregard Three," said Maddy, noting the fabric-constructed image of a farm boy pointing to the sky.

"And there, high on the right side, is the shooting star," noted Cookie. "This is the only visual record of the Madison Meteorite."

Like the fulcrum of an imaginary seesaw, a grain silo divided the picture. In this two-dimensional representation, the structure clearly stood in the path of the fireball.

A laminated plaque explained: "*Mary Louise Madison's Shooting Star Quilt memorialized a meteor storm that took place in northeastern Indiana in 1896. This quilt has been compared with the Bible Quilt 1886 and Pictorial Quilt 1898, creations by former slave Harriet Powers. The Powers quilts are considered among the finest examples of nineteenth-century Southern quilting. The Shooting Star Quilt was a Midwestern equivalent.*"

"There you have it," said Maddy, "everything that's known about that old space rock. Beau Three found it after it landed on the old Madison farm. Word of mouth said it knocked down the silo in the process."

"And killed a guy," added Bootsie.

"We don't know that for sure," said Maddy.

"If your hubby doesn't share his father's diary, we'll never know the full story," sighed Cookie.

"Granny Crackleton confirmed that it hit someone," Lizzie reminded them.

"That old woman's crazy as a June bug in a jar," Cookie said. "She's not what I'd call a reliable source."

"I thought you were big on oral history." Lizzie sounded defensive. She'd driven all way out to Cuckoo Crossing to interview the old crone. So much for self-initiative.

"You've got to question oral history from someone whose family tree is so inbred you can't tell whether it's oak or ash."

"Are all those stories about Cuckoo Crossing true?" asked Bootsie.

Cookie sniffed haughtily. "I've got genealogy charts on several of the folks who live up there. Gives credibility to that old country-western song, 'I'm My Own Grandpa.'"

"Just because Granny Crackleton's crazy doesn't mean she's not telling the truth," argued Lizzie. "She said she got the story directly from Beauregard Madison III. She was about twelve years old at the time; Beau's dad was about 50."

"I believe her," said Bootsie. "That rumor about the meteorite killing somebody's been around a long time. And where there's smoke there's fire."

"I wonder how the Indiana State Museum got hold of this quilt," mused Maddy. "It rightfully belongs to the Madison family."

"Now, now," chastised her friend Cookie. "You know if you had it, you'd donate it to the Historical Society — just like you made Beau do with the meteorite."

"True."

They paused to study the *Shooting Star Quilt*, taking in all the details. Farm boy. Silo. Heavenly manifestation.

"Wait a sec," muttered Lizzie. "Is that a man's face at the top of the silo?" She had extraordinary visual acuity. Always aced the eye tests, scoring well above average at 20/10. What's called super sight.

"I don't see anything," said Bootsie, squinting at the quilt.

Cookie fished her distance glasses from her purse.

"Me either," she said, peering up at the colorful quilt.

"Where?" asked Maddy.

"At the top of the silo in that little window."

"Window? That's probably an air vent. Looks blank to me."

"No, there's a pattern of threads, as if Mary Louise Madison started to sew in a face but didn't finish."

"You're seeing things," admonished Bootsie, drawing a blank.

"Lizzie dear, you're as cuckoo as Granny Crackleton," sighed Cookie, rolling her eyes.

"If we could only get closer . . ." Maddy shook her head.

"Grammy, we can," said Aggie.

"How dear? That quilt's twenty-feet-high on the wall."

"N'yen has a telescope."

The boy perked up. "Yes, let's test it out. Looking through the lens of my AstroMaster 114EQ will be like viewing the quilt from inches away."

"Really?" said Bootsie, dubious.

"I'll show you." He extended the 1.25-inch steel tube legs of the tripod and mounted the reflector telescope with its large 114mm coated glass mirror on top. Angling it upward, he focused on the silo in the quilt. "Hmm, here we go."

"Hold up there, young man!" came the stern voice of a museum docent. A short guy in a starched white shirt; a stern face. "No photography allowed in here."

N'yen looked up, irritated. "This isn't a camera; it's a telescope. There aren't any rules against stargazing in here, are there?"

"W-well, uh, I guess that's true," sputtered the museum volunteer. This was a first for him, a telescope inside the museum. "All right, go ahead as long as there's no camera attached," he said, trying to muster a semblance of authority.

"Whatever," waved N'yen, turning back to the AstroMaster. He fiddled with its mount controls and adjusted the 10mm eyepiece. However, instead of focusing on Saturn's moons or the Orion Nebula he turned the 269x magnification to the details of the quilt where the silo was stitched onto the dark blue background.

"What d'you see?" nudged Aggie. Eager.

"Hey, let me get this right," he shushed his cousin.

Maddy leaned closer. "Is there anything there?"

"Yeah, threads outlining the face of a man."

"Told you," said Lizzie.

"Ha!" exclaimed Cookie triumphantly. As if she'd seen it all along. "Proof that Beauregard Hollingsworth Madison III was not alone out there with that meteorite."

"Maybe when it hit the silo, it killed the guy inside," theorized Bootsie, as if she had solved a century-old crime all by herself.

"Let's not get ahead of ourselves," cautioned Maddy. "Just because Mary Louise Madison started to stitch in the image of a man in the silo doesn't mean anybody got killed."

"Of course it does," argued Bootsie. "We know the meteorite hit the silo. If anybody was in it he got pulverized."

"Not necessarily."

"If somebody got killed," Aggie said reasonably, "what happened to the body?"

"That's right, there were no funeral announcements in the *Burpyville Gazette* in the fall of 1896 for anyone bopped by a rock out of the sky," Maddy recalled.

"So what happened to the dead body?" asked Lizzie.

"We still don't know that there was one," Maddy insisted.

~ ~ ~

Getting back to Caruthers Corners late in the afternoon, the entourage decided to stop at Cozy Café for pie and coffee. Watermelon milkshakes for the kids. Maisie Walters was working the tables. She had worked here as a waitress since high school and liked to keep her hand in.

"Hi, Sis," she greeted Maddy.

"Uh, hello there," replied Maddy. It took some getting used to, the idea that she and Maisie were fraternal twins. Discovering you were a secret love child was hard to accept, even if the revelation came with a large inheritance.

Clustering in the corner booth (the one designed to hold five but could do six if you pulled up an extra chair) the Quilters Clubbers continued to discuss the 1896 meteorite. Finding the thread outline of a face in the silo on the *Shooting Star Quilt* supported the theory that the falling space debris had killed someone.

"But what happened to the dead guy?" Aggie insisted. She had inherited a sense of logic from her grandmother. That Greek guy Aristotle had nothing on Madelyn Agnes Madison or her granddaughter.

"Maybe the meteorite didn't kill him. The earth's

atmosphere slows them down so some don't land very hard if they've reached terminal velocity," explained N'yen, as if he were talking about what makes an apple fall.

"That's a thought," said Bootsie. "Maybe the fellow was only injured and crawled off to recover."

"If that happened, don't you think the guy would have been bragging about how he got hit by a falling star?" argued Lizzie. "I know I would've."

"That's right," Cookie agreed. "We'd find a story about it in one of those old papers on microfiche. Nobody would keep something like that to themselves."

Bootsie sipped at her high-octane coffee. "Well, if somebody got killed, Beau's father certainly kept *that* to himself."

"Apples and oranges," said Maddy. "Surviving a meteorite is something you'd boast about. Witnessing a guy get killed might be a different story."

"Wouldn't Beau's dad have told the guy's family?" said Cookie. "That would be the decent thing to do."

"People behave in strange ways," Maddy shrugged. Feeling defensive of her husband's father.

"The squib in the newspaper said the old silo got knocked down. Somebody up top would've been killed for sure," Lizzie stuck to Granny Crackleton's story.

"Was it ever rebuilt?" asked Maisie as she refilled their coffee cups.

"Was what rebuilt?" asked Bootsie, not following the waitress's line of thought.

"The silo. Was it ever rebuilt?"

"No," replied Cookie, the historian. "There's still a

pile of stones out there on what used to be the Madison farm."

Maisie shrugged, spilling a little coffee. "Simple then. The body's underneath all the rubble."

"Why didn't I think of that?" said Maddy. Suddenly realizing her sister possessed the same sense of logic as she did. They were swimming in the same gene pool.

CHAPTER NINETEEN

Faux George Washington

Fatty Johnson and his brother Clovis were related to the Jinkses on their mother's side of the family, but a few generations back the Johnsons also had married into the Crackleton clan. Perhaps that explained Clovis being a few sandwiches short of a picnic.

No wonder Fatty was pushing this Ferdinand Aloysius Jinks Heritage Society. It was the family's only claim to fame. Lineage with the Crackletons was nothing to brag about. As local schoolchildren liked to chant, the Crackletons were "cuckoo for Cocoa Puffs."

Fatty hired an ambulance-chasing lawyer ("Let Attorney Lester Reid tear up your speeding ticket!") over in Burpyville to set up the Jinks Heritage Society as a 501(c)3 and to petition the Caruthers Corners town council for permission to erect a statue of his ancestor in the square in front of the Town Hall. Since there were already bronze statues of Jacob Caruthers and Beauregard Madison in the park, it was only fair that the town council grant the request.

Permission was given in a 4 to 3 vote.

However, as it turned out, after paying his lawyer, Fatty didn't have enough money left to commission a statue of Ferdinand Aloysius Jinks. In desperation, he purchased a statue from a town park that was being closed in Southern Illinois. Unfortunately, it was a likeness of George Washington and despite Fatty putting his forbearer's name on a plaque at its base there was no fooling anyone. He was forced to remove the false identification and let it stand as the father of our country. The town moved it next to the Post Office on Fourth Avenue.

The Ferdinand Aloysius Jinks Heritage Society was back to square one.

~ ~ ~

Chief Jim Purdue made an inquiry with a friend at the FBI office in Indy about the Treasury Agent who was asking his cousin Bobby Ray for $10,000,000 in "special fees." Special Agent Neil Wannamaker got back to him with an inch-thick file on one Elbert Gregory Garrison Ignatius Ettelman (A/K/A Eggie Ettelman). The man was a small-time grifter with a long rap sheet. He had come to the FBI's attention a few years ago for trying to sell counterfeit War Bonds. That had netted him six months in the federal prison at Terre Haute.

Bobby Ray agreed to participate in a sting operation jointly conducted by the Caruthers Corners Police Department and the FBI. Posing as an agent of the US Treasury Department was a federal offence. So Bobby Ray told Ettelman that he would deliver the $10,000,000 in cash as requested.

For the sting, the FBI supplied fake bales of money. Ten million dollars in $100 bills (or their ersatz equivalent) weighs about 220 pounds and takes up 40 cubic feet. Much more than one man could carry. Ettelman would need a truck.

A time for the pickup was set: 10 a.m. on Saturday at Caruthers Corners Savings & Loan. The bank guard would haul it out on a dolly. The Feebies would have agents in place, two outside looking inconspicuous in cars, two inside pretending to be customers. A video guy would be recording the transfer from a panel truck parked across the street.

Eggie Ettelman didn't have a chance.

~ ~ ~

"Wait!" cried Eggie. "Don't shoot."

He was surrounded by FBI agents, although none actually had a gun in hand. Special Agent Neil Wanamaker stepped forward and said, "You're under arrest for impersonating a US Treasury Agent and attempted extortion. Anything you say may be held against you ..." *Et cetera, et cetera.*

Eggie looked glum. His vision of riches was fading with each word of the Mirandizing by the man known in law enforcement circles as Neil the Nailer.

Police Chief Jim Purdue breathed a sigh. Another bad guy off the street. And his cousin Bobby Ray owed him a big one, having saved the idiot from taking a $10-million haircut. Maybe as thanks the flamboyant millionaire would help fund a new wing for the police station. Having poured money into a retirement home for circus people, a petting zoo, the new museum, and the Historical Society, it was about time he helped the town's administrative functions.

"Hold on, boys," Eggie Ettelman was saying. "I wanna cut a deal. I can help you solve a murder if you go easy on me. What's a little con game compared to a cold-blooded killer on the loose."

"Local homicides are not the jurisdiction of the federal government," replied Special Agent

Wannamaker as he put the cuffs on Eggie. "You got nothing to trade."

"Wait a minute," Chief Purdue stepped forward. "What murder you talking about, Mr. Ettelman?"

"That fellow who got his head bashed in couple weeks ago. I know who done it."

"The flower shop murder?"

"Yeah, that's the one. Myron Madison, or whatever his name was. I can ID the killer for you."

"Care to make a statement about that?"

"Only if I get something in return."

Chief Purdue glanced at Neil Wannamaker. "I can't intercede in a federal criminal proceeding, but I'll put in a good word for you if you provide useful information in solving this recent murder. I'm sure the judge would take your cooperation into consideration."

Eggie shook his head. "Naw, I want more than that."

"Hmm. I believe I can get Bobby Ray Purdue to say he misunderstood your claiming to be a Treasury officer. That you were merely trying to raise money for charity."

"Hey –" protested Neil Wannamaker.

"Murder trumps a con game," Jim Purdue apologized. "I knew the deceased. And Bobby Ray is my first cousin. He'll play it whatever way I say." The policeman turned to the defrauded millionaire. "Right, Bobby Ray?"

The man in the gold lame suit shrugged. "Your call, cuz."

"This stinks," complained the FBI agent, leaning close so his men wouldn't hear. "But I'll reduce the charge to attempted extortion and recommend a light sentence if he gives you a good name."

The police chief nodded. "Thanks, Neil."

"You owe me, don't you forget that," the agent hissed.

Chief Purdue turned to Eggie. "Okay, you little scumbag, you've got one chance to get off with a lighter sentence, but I want a name right now."

"And I get a pass?"

"No, just less jail time. Take it or leave it."

"I'll take it," said Eggie.

CHAPTER TWENTY

A Jon Boat on the Wabash

Beauregard Madison didn't heed much to warnings. Beau had been a grunt during the Vietnam War, got used to his life being in danger. He'd been shot at by Viet Cong, had Soviet-made PMK-40s go off next to him, once stepped on a bamboo punji stick. A total of 58,220 US servicemen died in that conflict. He was lucky to have survived. Beau still had bad dreams.

Despite Police Chief Jim Purdue's admonitions, he went fishing as usual on Saturday with N'yen and Edgar Ridenour. Edgar's flat-bottomed jon boat drifted down the Wabash as if in slow motion. Dappled sunlight streamed through the overhead trees. They were using dough balls soaked in cherry Kool-Aid as bait, this being Jim's suggestion.

Their quest for the elusive Big Calvin had been suspended, even though they were near the bridge where the catfish was said to lurk. Edgar was half-dozing, barely guiding the boat. Beau was reading a clever murder mystery titled *Heat Until Boiling* by Maryjane Elizabeth Jones. N'yen was catching minnows with a net. A lazy hazy crazy day, nothing to do but relax.

As the boat approached the bridge for Highway 101, Beau glanced up from his paperback book, a motion catching his eye. Somebody on the bridge. That was unusual, for this stretch of highway was fairly deserted, no nearby commercial buildings, few farmhouses, just rolling pastureland farmed by the Amish. This area of Indiana claimed the largest population of Amish outside of Pennsylvania.

Beau started to look up.

"Grampy, d'you want to look for meteor showers tonight with my new telescope?" N'yen interrupted his reverie. The boy was still excited over his Celestron AstroMaster 114EQ, saying he might just become an astronomer when he grew up. Last week it was a robotics engineer. The week before that, a paleontologist.

Ka-thunk!

A cement block hit the boat a few inches from where Beau sat, as sudden as a comet out of the sky. The impact split the aluminum seam in the center of the hull and water began to seep in.

"What the –?" shouted Edgar, coming awake.

"Abandon ship!" yelled N'yen, jumping overboard into the murky water of the Wabash. Fortunately, he could swim. The 503-mile-long waterway flows southwest across northern and central Indiana to southern Illinois, where it forms the Illinois-Indiana border, then drains into the Ohio River.

The flat-bottom boat was all-but-untippable, but as Beau and Edgar shifted their weight to climb over the side, the craft overturned, dumping them and their fishing gear into the water. Although erosion from farming has made parts of the river shallow, the Wabash used to accommodate steamships. Here at the bridge was a deep spot, but they were able to dog-paddle to the shore.

"What happened?" asked Edgar, having been asleep when the missile struck his boat.

"Some jasper tried to coldcock me with a cement block. He was up there on the bridge."

Edgar surveyed the concrete span. "Think he's still up there? If so, I'm going to kick his butt."

"He's gone," said N'yen. "I heard a car drive away."

"Did you get a look at the car?" asked his grandfather.

"Not from down here."

"I can't believe the so-and-so sunk my boat. That Grizzly MVX was almost new. Set me back nearly nine grand."

"Yeah, a shame," commiserated Beau. "Tracker makes a good jon boat."

Edgar turned to his friend. "You say he was trying to drop a cement block on your head?"

"Sure looked like it. Missed me by a whisker."

"Then you oughta pay for a new boat. Wouldn't have been sunk if you weren't riding in it."

"Hold on there, Edgar. I can't help it some nutjob is trying to kill off my entire family. Besides, your boat was insured. You told me you bought a policy from Allstate."

"Guess it is," Edgar acquiesced. "I'm just rattled over being in the line of fire. You went to 'Nam, but I was 4-F on account of my flat feet."

N'yen spoke up. "My real dad's brother had flat feet. But he was still a colonel in the National Liberation Front of the *Kháng chién chóng Mý.*"

"*Kháng chién* what?"

"The Resistance War Against America."

"The Vietnam War," explained Beau.

"Hey, you little insurgent, I thought *you* were born in America," said Edgar.

"I was. But my uncle wasn't."

CHAPTER TWENTY-ONE

The Forgotten Silo

The Quilters Club decided to inspect the rubble that used to be the Madison farm's silo. Boyd Aitkens – who now owned the land – told them they could find it on that patch of pastureland west of Gruesome Gorge State Park.

They parked on the dirt road that ran parallel to a white-painted fence. Maddy and her friends piled out of the SUV, Aggie behind them. Being Saturday, she was out of school. Aggie's dog Tige jumped around like a whirligig, chasing bugs and other imaginary prey.

A Land Rover pulled up behind Maddy's Toyota Sequoia, Dr. Howard Carvel Oakman at the wheel. The paleontologist and his wife now worked for the Perricock Museum of Science & History. He had agreed to come along to help them look for bones. After all, that was his thing.

"Which way to the old silo?" asked Maddy.

"Boyd said it was located in the middle of the field," Cookie told them. She'd put in a call to the farmer, asking permission to poke around the old ruins.

"Middle of the field? You mean that clump of bushes?" asked Bootsie. The pasture was flat and grassy, but in the center was a small briar patch. There seemed to be a pile of stones among the tangled growth.

"Looks like it," nodded Maddy.

"May as well check that clump of bushes out," said Howie Oakman, climbing over the fence and walking across the expanse of grass toward the briars.

"Any bulls in there?" asked Lizzie nervously.

"A few cows, no bulls," said Cookie. "I asked Boyd."

"I don't like cows," said Lizzie.

"They won't bother you, Aunt Lizzie," said Aggie, following the others into the field. Tige raced on ahead, yipping as he chased after the paleontologist.

Lizzie glanced down at her shoes. "I'm wearing high heels," the redhead whined. "I'm not sure I can walk across the pasture in them."

"I told you to wear tennis shoes," chided Bootsie, hoisting herself over the top rail of the fence with great effort.

"Wait here if you want," said Maddy. "This is probably a wild goose chase anyway."

"Hey," Cookie interjected. "What do you mean, wild goose chase? It was your twin sister who suggested we poke around the ruins of the old silo."

"We're only *fraternal* twins," said Maddy defensively.

"Hurry up, Grammy," called Aggie. "I can see a pile of rocks."

Tige barked with what seemed like affirmation.

"This looks like the right spot," shouted Howie Oakman, standing at the edge of the briar patch. "Pile of stones here."

Maddy and Cookie crossed the field with Bootsie huffing along behind them. Lizzie grumbled as she kicked off her shoes and started climbing the fence. Aggie and her dog had joined Howie Oakman by now.

Everyone gathered at the bushy area, carefully keeping to the mown grass. The granite slabs were scattered like children's blocks. Sharp right angles pointed in all directions. Weeds grew between the blocks. Prickly briars made it difficult to get to the pile of rocks.

"Stand back," warned Howie Oakman as he produced a machete from his backpack and began hacking at the briars, clearing a path to the ruins of the collapsed silo.

"Do you think a meteorite actually knocked down this old silo?" asked Maddy.

"Not my area of expertise," said Oakman. "I'm just here to help you look for bones. I'm pretty good at that." He laid aside his machete and fished a short crowbar from the backpack. Hooking it under a boulder, he pried a squarish stone away from the one under it. Then he moved to the next. And the next.

If there had been any grain in the old stone silo, it was long gone – blown away by the winds, eaten by the birds. A few strands of wheat grew between the rocks. But mostly briars.

"What can we do to help?" queried Maddy, feeling awkward about standing there and twiddling her thumbs while the younger man toiled.

"Nothing, Mrs. Madison. I've got this. I'm used to digging for dinosaur bones in the Mesozoic strata of hot and dusty South Dakota. A cow pasture in Indiana is a breeze compared to that."

~ ~ ~

Boyd Aitken drove out to his back pasture to see how those busybody women were coming with their search of the old silo ruins. He raised a few beef cattle – mostly Aberdeen and Hereford – in this pasture, although his main business was growing watermelons. He was by far the biggest melon producer in the county.

He parked his Bronco behind the Toyota and Land Rover, climbed over the white wooden fence, and trudged across the pasture, his feet leaving impressions in the soft canary grass. Indiana has approximately 762,619 acres of pastureland that provides forage for beef cattle, dairy cattle, sheep, goats, horses, and other types of domestic livestock.

"Hello there," he called out to the group in the middle of the green field. "Having any luck?"

"Oh, hello there, Boyd," responded Maddy. "Nothing yet. This may be a wild goose chase."

The watermelon farmer surveyed their excavation. Stones had been moved aside to get at the center of the pile. "I always heard that meteorite landed somewhere in this field. You think it's true?"

"Yes," said Cookie. "We've got the meteorite. It came down somewhere around here."

"And you think it knocked down this old silo?"

"That's the legend."

"So what are you looking for?" Aitkens wanted to know. "Another meteorite?"

"No," said Maddy. "A skeleton."

Chapter Twenty-Two

Powerball Winner

Fatty Johnson and his brother Clovis had blown their money on the statue of George Washington. Too bad the town wouldn't let them put Ferdinand Jinks's name on it and pass the effigy off as their beloved ancestor. The mayor was being difficult, probably because he was married to a Madison.

He'd have to remember to put the mayor on his People to Get Even With List. If President Trump could have an Enemies List, so could he.

Fatty had been offered a good buy on a statute of Jefferson Davis from a town in South Carolina. They were pulling down all those homages to the Confederacy, a PC movement that was stripping the South of its past in an effort to forget that slavery ever happened. Ol' Jeff Davis wasn't as recognizable as George Washington and might get by as a substitute for his great-great-grandfather.

Kind of a historical identity theft, as it were.

The cost: Two grand plus shipping.

Unfortunately, the Ferdinand Aloysius Jinks Heritage Society was out of funds.

The Johnson family wasn't wealthy. Fatty lived on disability, a supposed back injury from falling off that Christmas float back in 2002. As for Clovis, he couldn't hold a job. And their mother survived on a widow's pension from the Post Office (their dad had been a mailman).

Fatty's uncle, Tall Paul Johnson, had died of pneumonia a few years back but his widow was still around, living at that home for retired circus folks. She had been a tattooed lady with a carnival. Problem was, she'd given all her money to an animal rescue organization.

Fatty's aunt, an elderly woman named Hortense Eleanor Whitaker, lived over in Burpyville. It was said she had oodles of money, but she was known to be tightfisted. Not much chance of getting a nickel out of Aunt Hortense.

Clovis suggested they rob a bank, but he wasn't entirely right in the head. That Crackleton blood in the veins, no doubt. Clovis had poor impulse control.

But maybe that was a way to get the money – from the Crackleton side of the family. Everybody knew Granny Crackleton's son Jebediah was rich. He'd won the state lottery a couple of years ago. The odds of winning the Powerball jackpot are one in 292,201,338. But of all the 44 participating states, Indiana has had the most Powerball winners since the game launched in 1992.

Jeb won $1 million in the Powerball Quick Pick on a 5/5 match. He'd bought the $2 ticket at the family's general store in Crackleton Crossing. People had accused him of hanky-panky, but no one could prove that he and his six-fingered son Dub had rigged the system.

While Dub was less than five feet tall, his father Jeb was a giant, rivaling Tall Paul Johnson's legendary 7-foot stature, shorter by only one inch. With Tall Paul's passing, Jeb officially had become the tallest man in

Indiana. The state record was still held by John Wright, an Anderson resident who died in 1889. At 8 feet (243.8 cm), he was considered the tallest man in the United States at the time.

After winning Powerball, Jeb Crackleton had set up an unofficial loan shark business. He had no trouble collecting on debts, for nobody wanted the Crackleton clan knocking on the door. His other two sons were more like a pack of jackals than debt collectors. Scary, to say the least.

Fatty figured Jeb might give him a break, being related and all. Surely he would agree that erecting a statue to Ferdinand Jinks was a worthy cause. And cousin Jeb had the two thousand dollars needed to buy the statue.

~ ~ ~

Edgar dropped Beau and his grandson at their home on Melon Pickers Row. His boat and fishing tackle were at the bottom of the Wabash River. They had salvaged the big blue Igloo drink cooler and Beau's boonie hat. Their clothes had almost dried by the time they got back to town.

First thing Beau did was phone the police station to report the cement block thrown off the bridge, but Jim Purdue was "out on a big case," according the dispatcher Myrtle Dobbler. Beau explained his problem, but he wasn't sure she got it. She assured him the Chief would get back to him in due course.

Beau dreaded telling his wife. Maddy would go into Mother Hen mode. Yet there was no choice, for she might be in danger. Maybe Tilly and Aggie too.

He called the mayor's office and got his son-in-law on

the phone. Mark the Shark was upset with the news, seeing a pattern emerge – Mycroft, Freddie, Bill, himself, now Beau. Needless to say, he was concerned for the safety of his wife and daughter.

Next Beau went up to the attic and unlocked his old US Army field trunk, a relic from his Vietnam days. The green wooden box held his old dress uniform, a pair of canvas-and-leather jungle boots, a Vietnamese silk painting that showed a hut and palm trees, and a Colt M1911A1 pistol.

He took out the pistol and a box of .45 ammo. A single-action, semi-automatic, magazine-fed handgun designed by John Browning, the M1911 was the standard-issue sidearm for the US Army from 1911 to 1986. He'd brought it back from the war.

Carrying the .45 downstairs, he loaded the magazine with cartridges and laid it on the table near the front door where he usually put the mail.

"Grampy, why've you got a gun?" N'yen asked, eyes wide.

"Better safe than sorry," he said, patting the boy affectionately on the head. "Don't want any more cement blocks coming our way."

"I can lay some booby traps in the front yard," said N'yen, getting into the swing of things. "I've been reading up on how to make landmines after seeing that pressure cooker bomb that blew up the fire truck."

"Bet you have," said his grandfather.

"And we could dig a *trou de loup*. You know, a tiger pit with punji sticks."

"Hold up, partner. You're sounding like a one-man killing machine."

"One boy. Remember, I'm only twelve."

"That may be a little young to practice the art of booby trapping."

"My uncle was making Keepsake-Lose-Hand and Two-Step-Charlie traps when he was eight. He started out fighting with the Viét Minh against the French. Then against the Americans. Us Americans, I mean. But I wasn't born at the time."

"I'll have to meet your uncle some day."

"Anytime you like, Grampy. Uncle Võ lives in Cleveland. He owns a very popular Thai restaurant there."

"Thai? But he's Vietnamese."

"There were too many Vietnamese restaurants on his side of town. So he started a place to eat called Thai U Up. People line up at the door."

"How come Võ didn't take you when your parents died?"

"He was much too busy for a grasshopper like me. I'm much better off with you, Grampy. Being retired, you have time to take me fishing."

Chapter Twenty-Three

Boning Up

Howard Oakman had moved quite a few stone blocks aside. Boyd Aitken joined him in the excavation. By now they were about three feet down in the pile of rubble. They had uncovered a few wooden beams and metal roofing shingles. After 121 years, the wood had pretty much rotted away, and the shingles were blood-red with rust.

The farmer saw it first. "Is that a bone?" Boyd Aitkens said, stepping back and pointing.

Howie Oakman leaned closer, inspected what looked like a yellowed stick showing between two granite boulders. "A humerus," he identified it.

"A what?" asked Lizzie.

"A human arm bone," he explained. "Looks pretty well preserved. Buried under these stones kept predators away, protected it from the weather."

"But isn't the arm bone connected to the ...?" said Maddy.

"Yes, I can see a radius and ulna just below it. Pretty much the whole arm. A left one, I'd say. But I'm more used to piecing together dinosaurs than people."

"How'd that arm get here?" said Boyd Aitkens, staring at the hole.

"Probably came with the rest of the dead body," replied the paleontologist, sporting a wry grin.

Maddy said, "This is what we were looking for,

Boyd. The remains of a man killed by the meteorite of 1896. Just like the legend told us."

"I thought that was an old wives tale. Something Granny Crackleton made up to scare children."

"More likely this poor fellow was killed when the meteorite hit the silo and caused it to collapse on him," clarified Cookie. "Professor Claypool from the University of Indiana Bloomington says it's extremely rare that someone actually might get struck by a meteorite."

"I don't like having had a dead body out here on my property all these years and not knowing about it," Aitkens grumbled. "Spooky, that's what it is."

"Matter of fact, if you dug up this pasture you'd likely find a few Potawatomi bones too," said Oakman. He was referring to the indigenous people who had lived here when the land was known as Indian Territory.

"My field hands plow up a lot of arrowheads, some pottery."

"I know what to do when I dig up a Tyrannosaurus bone," said the paleontologist. "But I'm not sure what to do about a human's."

Bootsie was picking briars out of her knit dress. "Simple," she said. "We call my husband."

~ ~ ~

Chief Jim Purdue turned on his Sony micro recorder and held it out to catch Eggie's words. "If you want the deal, tell me who killed Mycroft Madison," he said gruffly.

"Uh, I don't know the guy's name, but I saw him do it."

"No name?"

"I can ID him, no question about it."

"You're sure about that?"

"Yeah, no question."

"And you saw him do it?"

"That's right. I went over to that flower shop to buy a carnation for my lapel. Wanted to look slick, like a Treasury Agent."

"Treasury Agents don't wear flowers in their lapels," said Neil Wannamaker.

"They don't? How would I know? I've never met one."

Chief Purdue continued, "Tell me how you happened to witness the murder?"

Eggie seemed eager to talk. "Well, it occurred to me I might find a discarded carnation out back," he said, "something thrown out from the previous day. Save me a buck or two. So I walked around the building toward a trash barrel next to a big white truck. I could see flowers sticking out of the barrel – roses and buttercups and stuff like that. About then I heard voices inside the truck and I thought about taking off, but as I started to step back there came a thunk and a groan. That's when I saw a guy jump out of the truck and take off running. I peeked into the truck and saw a man laying there on the floor. His head was bloody, so I didn't stick around."

"You didn't check to see if he was simply injured?"

"No, I was scared. Afraid I'd get blamed. I have a few convictions for fraud, check kiting, and bar fights. But you likely know that by now."

The police chief scowled, the wrinkles framing his

mouth like parentheses. "You sure you didn't bang the guy on the head to rob him?"

"No way. You won't find my fingerprints in that refrigerator truck or on the murder weapon."

"Murder weapon?"

Eggie looked worried. "There was a bag of rocks beside the body. It had blood on it."

"You identifying the murder weapon only proves you were there," accused the police chief. "We haven't released that info yet."

"I told you I saw the murderer. I can pick him out of a lineup."

"You've gotta give me more than that, pal," said the police chief. "That's nothing I can go on. I'm gonna have to leave you to the feds."

"Wait —"

Special Agent Wannamaker cut him off. "We're taking you into custody, Mr. Ettelman. The charges are extortion and impersonating a federal officer." He turned to the police chief. "We'll hold him down in Indy. You want to do a picture lineup, come on down. If he identifies the murderer, we can revisit the charges. If not, I've got a room reserved for him down in Terre Haut."

~ ~ ~

Police Chief Jim Purdue didn't have a chance to sit down. The minute he stepped inside the station door Myrtle Dobbler besieged him with a handful of pink message slips. "Everybody's looking for you," she admonished. "Where in heaven's name have you been?"

"Doing my job. I don't report to you, Myrtle."

"No sir, but I'm trying to do my job too. And that's

difficult when you disappear and don't answer the radio or your cell phone."

"I didn't disappear. I told you I was meeting the FBI to make an arrest."

"Yes sir. Your cousin wants you to call him."

"I just left Bobby Ray ten minutes ago."

"Can't help that. He's called twice in the last three minutes."

As if on cue, the phone on Myrtle's desk started to ring.

"You wife called. Says to call her cell phone right away."

"What's the rush? Has she found a dead body or something?"

"A skeleton," Myrtle replied.

"What –?"

"And Beau Madison asked that you call him. Said there was an attempt on his life."

"Holy moly. Anything else?"

"The mayor wants police protection for his family. Petie Hitzer arrested a state senator for speeding. Daniel Sokolowski reported a break-in. And Jasper Beanie turned himself in for drunk and disorderly. Jasper's sleeping it off as usual in holding cell two."

"Sounds like a typical morning," he said. But Myrtle Dobbler didn't get the sarcasm.

PART TWO

The Dead Man

"Catch a falling star and put it in your pocket/
Never let it fade away/
Catch a falling star and put it in your pocket/
Save it for a rainy day."

- Paul Vance and Les Pockriss, 1957,
recorded by Perry Como

Chapter Twenty-Four

Piecing It Together

Agnes Millicent Tidemore knew her cousin N'yen would be bummed that he wasn't here to watch the excavation. Only two weeks ago he was talking about becoming a paleontologist when he grew up. And now he was missing the chance to watch Dr. Howard Carvel Oakman of the Perricock Science & History Museum uncover a century-old skeleton from Boyd Aitkens's pasture.

Bootsie Purdue had phoned her husband and he had phoned the coroner. Doc Medford had just arrived and he and Howie Oakman were extracting the yellowed bones from the rocks and laying them out in the shape of a human on a blue tarp. It was fascinating to watch. Who knew a person had so many bones in them? 206 in an adult, according to Doc Medford.

Aggie's grandmother had gathered the Quilters Club around her for a powwow. They were clustered about fifteen feet from the ruins of the old silo. All that was left to mark the spot of the structure was a tangle of briars and a pile of stone slabs.

Lizzie was complaining about a tear in her dress from the thorns. Apparently it was a designer original. The redhead was known to be the "fashion plate" of the group, fussy about her appearance.

Nevertheless, Liz Ridenour was the best quilter among them. She had become Aggie's personal mentor, teaching the girl how to make cross stitches, tunneling stitches, running stitches, and the essential quilter's knot. It was Lizzie who had spotted the thread outline of a face in the tower on the Pictorial Quilt at the Indiana State Museum. That was the first concrete evidence there was a second person present when Beauregard Madison III – Aggie's grandfather – discovered the 1896 meteorite.

The women where huddled close to the spot where that meteorite landed after crashing through the silo and collapsing it on that poor individual whose bones were being spread out on the tarp. Aggie inspected the pasture's smooth blanket of grass but no evidence of the meteorite's impact could be seen after more than a hundred years.

"Found a rusty belt buckle," she heard Howie Oakman say.

"Put it there on the side of the tarp," replied the coroner.

A few minutes later, Oakman said, "Here's a ring. Wide band, probably gold. Big ruby inset."

"Put it next to the buckle," directed the coroner.

Another half-hour and Aggie was starting to get fidgety. "How much longer?" she whined. The girl didn't have the patience of her cousin N'yen. He could sit and watch a butterfly flutter about the garden for hours.

"I think we're wrapped up here," muttered Doc Medford. "Don't see any more bones, although it looks like some small metatarsals and a clavicle are missing."

The mention of a ring had caught Maddy Madison's ear. "Mind if I look at that ring?" she called to Doc Medford. "It might help identify the body."

"No offense, Maddy, but I'd best hold it for the police chief to examine."

"I don't want to take it; just look at it."

"Yes, but –"

"Doc," Bootsie spoke up. "I'm sure Jim won't mind our simply looking at that old ring."

The coroner wasn't going to argue with the police chief's wife. Or the mayor's mother-in-law. He was an appointed official. "Go ahead, but be quick. I want to pack these bones up and take 'em back to the morgue." The "morgue" was actually a room at Yost & Yost Funeral Home next door to his doctor's office.

The four women crowded around the tarp. The bones formed the Halloween-like shape of a skeleton. To the side lay the ring and rusty belt buckle. "Big ruby," said Lizzie. "Must be worth a pretty penny."

"What can you tell from the bones?" Cookie asked the coroner.

He cleared his throat, as if about to give a lecture. "Male. About 5-foot-6 judging by the length of the femur. No apparent cause of death, although there is a crack in the skull. That was likely caused by the collapse of the structure, all those rocks falling on top of him. That might have killed him, or the weight of the rocks on his chest may have caused asphyxiation, or he could have been trapped and starved to death. Anybody's guess after all these years."

"Did you find any identification?" pressed Cookie.

"Nothing other than that belt buckle and ring."

Lizzie stared down at the rusty buckle. "That's just a generic belt buckle. Nothing to go on there."

"But the ring," said Maddy. "That might be a clue."

"We should let Mr. Sokolowski look at it," suggested Aggie. "He might have some ideas about it." Daniel Sokolowski was the elderly proprietor of Dan's Den of Antiquity, the trash and treasures shop on Main Street. He was knowledgeable about old jewelry and such.

"Sorry, young lady," said the coroner. "We have to maintain a chain of custody on this evidence. That ring and belt buckle gets turned over to the police."

Bootsie was not deterred. "I'll phone Dan and ask him to meet us at the police station. I'm sure my husband will appreciate the help."

Chapter Twenty-Five

The Ruby Ring

Dan Sokolowski hobbled into the police station, the squarish concrete building just up the street from his antiques shop. The octogenarian had snow-white hair and a bushy beard. He wore a plaid shirt and khaki pants. Despite his age, his posture was as erect as a flagpole. "Hello," he greeted Myrtle Dobbler in his distinct Eastern European accent. "The Chief's wife asked me to meet her here."

"Yes, she and her friends are in Chief Purdue's office," she waved a hand toward a closed door. "Go right in, Mr. Sokolowski. They're expecting you."

He nodded his thanks and slowly pushed the door open, cautiously sticking his head inside. He recognized the four members of the Quilters Club and young Agnes Tidemore. He'd consulted with them on solving mysteries in the past. Very clever women, in his opinion.

"Daniel, glad you're here," the police chief greeted him. "We found a big ruby ring on the hand of a dead body – well, a skeleton really. Been dead over a hundred years. We're hoping you might be able to tell us something about the ring. Might help us with identifying the deceased."

"I'll do my best," said Sokolowski.

Jim Purdue pulled out a small paper bag, the kind that might hold penny candy, and shook it over his desk. A dirt-encrusted ring tumbled onto the green ink blotter. "Here you go. Take a look."

"May I pick it up?"

"Sure. You can brush off the dirt if you like."

The antiques dealer scooped up the ring and balanced it in the palm of his hand. "I can tell you it's a male finger ring. Heavy. Probably pure gold." He pulled out a handkerchief and rubbed away the dirt. "Nice stone. A ruby. Looks real." He held it up to the light, then produced a jeweler's glass from his pocket and put it to his eye. "Hm, not a class ring; not a secret society insignia; not a wedding ring. Not a memory ring; not a signet ring; not a sewing ring."

"Sewing ring?" said Maddy. "What's that?"

"An early form of thimble which took the shape of a simple ring. They date back to the Han Dynasty in ancient China."

"Could it be a birthstone ring?" asked Lizzie.

"That's a possibility. The ruby usually means July with modern birthstones."

Cookie said, "This guy likely died in 1896."

Dan Sokolowski seemed to consider this. "That changes things. Prior to 1912 the ruby represented the month of December. What's more, the ruby is the gemstone for Capricorn. That's the Zodiac symbol for December 22 to January 21. So it is likely your person was born in December. But that's just a guess."

"Anything else?" asked Bootsie.

He looked through the jeweler's glass again, turning the ring around in his fingers. Examining the design, the inside of the band. "What have we here?" he said.

"What?" asked Chief Purdue, leaning forward.

"May I have some water?"

Aggie ran over to the water cooler and filled a paper cup. Sokolowski dipped the corner of his handkerchief into the water, then threaded it into the interior of the ring. It made a squeaking sound as he twisted it around the metal circle. "That's much better," he said. "Give me just a moment." He put his eye back to the jeweler's glass. "Yes, I can see it now. Four letters are engraved inside the band – ACEJ."

"ACEJ –?"

He studied the ring. "That is what I see. The letters A and C and E and J. Does that mean anything to you?"

"Not offhand," said Cookie. "But I'll try to match it against my genealogy charts."

"J," said Chief Purdue. "That could stand for Jinks or Johnson or Jaggi or Jenson."

"Or Jones," sighed his wife. "This is going to be like looking for a name in a can of alphabet soup."

~ ~ ~

As everyone filed from the police chief's office, Jim Purdue put a hand on Maddy's arm. "Before you go home –" he halted her.

"What?" She didn't like the anxious tone of his voice. "Has anything happened to Beau or N'yen?"

"Not exactly. Everybody's all right."

"Then what?"

"Somebody tried to drop a cement block on Beau's head ... but thank goodness the perp missed."

"Oh my. Somebody *is* trying to kill the entire Madison family."

"Looks like that might be the case," the police chief

admitted. "You could be in danger too, Maddy."

"How do we protect ourselves?"

"I'll have my deputies do extra patrols along Melon Pickers Row. And around the town square past the Taylor house." That's where Tilly and her family lived, the magnificent old Victorian where Maddy herself had been raised as a girl.

"Thank you, Jim. But will that be enough?"

"Well, Mark the Shark is hiring a private security firm for his family. Just till we catch this guy. You and Beau might consider doing the same. I can give you the name of a company out of Indy – Iron Fist Enterprises. Has a good reputation."

~ ~ ~

Jebediah Crackleton looked up as Fatty Johnson walked into the general store. Crackleton Crossing didn't get too many visitors from town. But this week it had been like Grand Central Station – first that redheaded woman, then Beau Madison's wife, and now Fatty.

While Jebediah's son Dub managed Crossroads Mercantile & Gas, Jeb himself kept daily office hours at a desk in the far corner. A bare light bulb dangling over his head, he doled out money at a 20 percent interest rate. The stark lighting gave him a sinister look, probably the intended effect. He ran his loan-sharking business with draconian glee.

"How can I help you?" Jeb greeted the corpulent visitor. "You need some money, Fatty?"

"Matter of fact, I do. But it's not for me."

"Is it for that idiot brother of yours?" asked Jed Crackleton, his long legs extending from under the desk. At almost seven-feet-tall he didn't fit normal furniture.

"No, not this time. It's for the honor of the Jinks family. Being you and me both trace our lineage back to ol' Ferdinand Jinks, I'm hoping we can talk about a donation to the cause ... not a loan."

Jed laughed, a derisive sound. "I don't do donations, you should know that."

"But in this case –"

"Ain't no case here to discuss. I don't give a dingleberry about the Jinks family name. Up here at the Crossing, we're Crackletons."

Fatty shifted his weight, making the floorboards groan. "As you know, I got Crackleton blood in me too. But we both trace our family tree back to Ferdinand Jinks. He deserves to be honored as a town founder. Them thieving Caruthers kin and those self-aggrandizing Madisons have stolen ol' Ferdie's rightful place in history."

"How much money d'you want? And what d'you want it for?" demanded Jed, banging his fist on his desk. The noise made his son Dub jump, almost falling off his stool behind the cash register. Fatty took a step back, uncertain how to proceed.

"Two thousand dollar would buy a bronze statue of Ferdinand Aloysius Jinks to go in the town square," blathered Fatty. "Something to remind people of his role in founding the town."

"Haw! Like I care about that stupid little town that shuns us Crackletons!"

"This is for posterity. I'm only talking two grand."

Jed Crackleton leaned forward, elbows on his desk.

He looked like a giant insect about to devour its prey. "I'll loan you the two thousand dollars, if you want. But interest is twenty percent a week compounded. Comes due in thirty days."

"I need more than thirty days to get donations coming in for the Ferdinand Aloysius Jinks Heritage Society."

"Sixty days then. But you have to pay the vig every week."

"E-every week?"

"You want the money or not?"

"Yes, it's for a good cause. But I think you could be a little more generous for a family project."

"The only family I care about is my mama Sarah an' my son Willard here. My twins can go to hell. El and Vis always got their hands out; them boys never hold down a steady job."

Barely visible from behind the cash register, Willard – better known as Dubya or simply Dub – waved to acknowledge his presence. His hand looked strange with the sixth finger sticking out like an extra thumb. "You can make a statue of me," cackled the tiny man. "Wouldn't take much bronze. Save you a bundle of money."

"You gotta be famous to get a statue in the park," muttered Fatty.

"Hey," said the little man, "people know who I am."

"Maybe in carnival freak shows. You got more fingers than an octopus."

Jeb spoke up. "Don't you make fun of my son if you want to borrow this money." The big man had counted out two thousand dollars in $20 bills, slapping them down on top of his desk. "Here you go. You want the moolah or not?"

"Okay, okay. But if I pay you back early the vig stops – right?"

"Sure, sure."

"Then I'd best order that statue. You'll be proud of our ancestor once he takes his place next to those memorials to Jacob Caruthers and Beauregard Madison."

"You don't like their families much, do you? Can't say as I blame you. Too hoity-toity for my taste."

"Not many Caruthers are left hereabouts. Good riddance to bad rubbish. And I'd be happy to see an end to the Madison dynasty too." You would have thought Fatty was a political wingnut talking about the Bushes or Clintons or Kennedys.

CHAPTER TWENTY-SIX

The Hamburglar Strikes

Sunday night Aggie was awakened by a low growl. Her dog always slept on the foot of her bed. She sat up in time to see the silhouette of Tige jump off the bed and race from the room. She could hear him barking all way down the stairs. He would wake up the entire household if he kept that up. Her sisters shared the room next to hers. She could hear Mandy start to cry.

Downstairs Tige was carrying on something terrible. Barking. Growling. Throwing himself against the back door. Had he gone mad? Rabies or something like that?

Or could someone be out there?

Aggie padded barefoot to the window and brushed back the curtain. A full moon bathed the backyard in a bluish light. She could see the shapes of the shrubbery and the flower garden and the big oak tree with her swing. Then she saw a dark figure cross the lawn and slip through the gate in the fence that ran along the alleyway.

A burglar?

~ ~ ~

Beau Madison came awake when he heard the scream. He snatched the M1911 off his nightstand and headed down the stairs. It sounded like it came from the backyard patio.

"What is it?" Maddy called after him.

"Go back to bed," he hissed. "I'll handle this."

Of course, she didn't.

By now young N'yen was up, padding down the hall in his Spider-Man pajamas. "I got him!" he shouted to his grandfather. "I got him!"

Beau flung open the back door, pistol at the ready. But no one was there.

"Don't go outside, Grampy," warned N'yen. "There's a trap on the steps."

"A trap?" Beau flipped the lights on. Light flooded the patio. He could see bloody tracks on the fieldstone, leading toward the gate in the fence.

N'yen caught his grandfather's arm, preventing him from stepping outside. "I laid a punji trap for the killer. Just like my Uncle Võ taught me. Sounded like I got him."

Beau stooped down to examine the back entrance. The boy had removed the middle step, leaving a hole filled with upright pencils, their sharpened tips pointing skyward. A couple of them were broken off, covered in bright red blood. In the dark the missing step would not have been apparent. The intruder had spiked himself on the bed of No. 2 pencils.

"Good job," said Beau. "But you'd best remove this trap before your Grammy steps on it."

"Simple. You just replace the top of the step. At night you remove it again. Keeps the house safe."

"Your Uncle Võ taught you this?"

"Well, this is a variation on his instructions. I had to improvise with the pencils."

"Are there other traps around here?" Beau looked right and left as if searching for landmines in Vietnam.

"Just one at the front door that I made using M-88 firecrackers left over from last Fourth of July. That was as close to a toe popper as I could come."

"How do you know about toe poppers?"

"Uncle Võ."

"Figures. You'd better remove it before Fritz Berber blows off his foot while delivering the mail today." Fritz had been their mailman for the past twenty years.

"Didn't think of that."

"We get a few door-to-door salesman too."

"They would be collateral damage," winked the boy as he headed toward the front door.

Beau continued to stare down at the bed of sharpened pencils. Someone *had* been trying to break into their house – the killer? – but had been greeted by a nasty surprise.

Might make Jim Purdue's job easier. He just had to look for a suspect who was limping. The blood indicated somebody had been injured. Those pencils would have jammed straight through the sole of a tennis shoe.

CHAPTER TWENTY-SEVEN

Santa Claus Is Real

Monday morning Police Chief Jim Purdue got a message from the Feds that Elbert Ettelman was ready to talk. So the Chief agreed to drive down to Indy and interview the prisoner at the FBI offices.

Maybe he'd get a straight story from the shifty little con man, now that he'd had time to cool his heels over the weekend in the Marion County jail. It wasn't a pleasant place to be incarcerated.

Eggie was waiting in an interrogation room. As a courtesy, Special Agent Neil Wannamaker had brought him from his jail cell to the FBI office for the meeting with Police Chief Purdue.

The man looked fairly pathetic, sitting there in his khaki pants and shirt, the official dress code for federal prisoners. With the nickname of Eggie, you'd expect him to have a round Humpty Dumpty physique – but no, he was slim and trim, in good shape for his 36 years. He went to the gym regularly. You could expect him to pump up like a muscleman, if he remained in prison, where lifting weights was a popular pastime.

Eggie looked up when Chief Purdue stepped into the room. The US Marshall who had accompanied him from his cell in the Marion County Jail on South Alabama Street took a chair in a far corner of the room, trying to be as unobtrusive as possible.

"How you doing, Elbert?" asked Jim Purdue.

"Call me Eggie. All my friends do."

"I'm not sure we qualify as friends," said Chief Purdue, taking a seat at the metal table, directly across from the prisoner. The room was small, no pictures on the walls, the only furniture being the table and four chairs.

"Whatever. Still call me Eggie."

"Okay, Eggie. You said you were willing to ID the killer of Mycroft Madison."

"That's right. But first I want a deal."

"What d'you have in mind?"

"That I walk on the con charge."

Chief Purdue pursed his lips. "Don't think that'll happen."

"Look, Bobby Ray's your cousin. All you gotta do is ask him to drop the charges, say it was all a misunderstanding, and I'll finger the murderer for you."

"Dunno. You're looking pretty good for that murderer role yourself."

"Bull hockey, I didn't kill nobody. Look at my rap sheet. You'll see I'm a penny-ante grifter, not a twist-your-cap guy."

"Trying to extort $10 million isn't exactly penny-ante."

"So I had ambitions ... can't blame me for going for the brass ring."

"Well, actually we can. That's why you're here."

"C'mon. Give me something if you want what I know."

Chief Purdue shrugged. "Eighteen months for attempted extortion. The Feds will drop the impersonating a Treasury Agent charge. Considering that plastic badge you flashed, it was a pretty poor impersonation at that."

"Okay, I'll take it." He smiled as if he'd just graduated from Trump U with a degree in *Art of the Deal*. Obviously unaware that Federal prisons offer much better accommodations than eighteen months in an underfunded state penitentiary.

"Deal," said Chief Purdue. He'd already worked out the plea bargain with Neil Wannamaker. The Feds didn't really want to reel in this minnow when there were bigger fish out there.

"Like I say, I don't know the guy's name, but he should be easy to identify."

"How so?"

"Well, he looked kinda like Santa Claus."

"Santa Claus? You're sure about that?"

"Yeah, fat. White beard."

"Maybe there is no Santa Claus. Are you sure *you* didn't bang the guy on the head to rob him?"

"No way. Now that I told you what the murderer looks like. He oughta be easy to find."

"Maybe he was wearing a disguise. Padding, fake beard. Or maybe you just made him up."

"No, honest. I saw him," Eggie Ettelman said. "Santa Claus is real."

~ ~ ~

That same day Mark the Shark and his father-in-law met in the Town Hall conference room with the head of Iron Fist Enterprises, the private security firm out of Indianapolis.

According to the man's business card, his name

was Drake Hammer. But Mark had checked him out, discovering that his birth name was actually Dean Ray Hammond and that he had an associate degree in criminal justice from Ball State University. Working as a bouncer at a strip club had led to acting as a bodyguard for local politicians. That had expanded into a full line of security services that ranged from installing alarm systems to background checks, from deprogramming cult followers to protecting visiting celebs.

"I'll post two men at each of your homes, one front, one back. All four are former Navy Seals with military assault training. They will be armed with Tasers and equipped with night-vision scopes. Nobody will get past them, believe you me."

"What's it cost?" asked Mark Tidemore.

"One thousand dollars a day per station. We're talking two security points – front and back – that's two grand a day for each of you."

"Rather expensive," noted Beau Madison, parsimonious at heart.

"True, but with luck it won't last long. I'd expect we'll snag this psycho within a week to ten days. Nut jobs like this are acting compulsively, can't resist the urge to carry out their agenda. He won't drag this out very long before trying again."

"He was at my house last night," said Beau.

"Mine too," added Mark.

"My point exactly," said Drake Hammer, a smile tilting the corners of his lips. At that moment he knew he had the lucrative assignment. He could drag this gig out for weeks on end without ever catching the bad guy.

No problem on that score. His men were more muscle than brains.

~ ~ ~

N'yen reluctantly removed the sharpened pencils and replaced the wooden step. His Grampy had assured him he wouldn't need the punji trap now that a security firm was going to be watching their house 24/7. The boy thought the extra barrier for an intruder couldn't hurt, but apparently there was a fear that some unsuspecting neighbor might pierce his foot on the sneaky little pitfall. One could get seriously hurt. A pencil could penetrate a rubber sole, embedding itself in a person's foot like a knife. That kind of injury might easily get infected. If gangrene sets in, one could loose a foot.

N'yen saw this as cheap home security.

Beau Madison saw it as potential for an expensive homeowner's lawsuit.

CHAPTER TWENTY-EIGHT

The Usual Suspect

"Only one person it could be," nodded Deputy Evers Gochnauer. "Fatty Johnson."

"Just because Eggie Ettelman said the murderer looked like Santa Claus doesn't prove it was Fatty," said Petie Hitzer. "There are plenty of fat people in this town. They eat too many fried cheese balls."

"No, I think the Chief's hunch is right about it being Fatty," continued Evers Gochnauer unabated. "Fatty used to be Santa Claus in the Christmas Parade. And he's fat and has a white beard."

"So is Karl Schaeffer. He wins the watermelon-eating contest every year. Probably weighs 300 pounds."

"Karl doesn't have a beard."

"How about Fatty's brother Clovis? He looks like a Mini Me – fat and with a white beard."

"Not a likely suspect. He hasn't got the brains to plan a murder."

"What about Jeff Brown. He took over as Santa in the Christmas parade."

"That's right, I almost forgot about Jeff," said Evers Gochnauer.

Petie Hitzer thought about it for a few minutes. "Naw, couldn't be. Jeff has the shape, but no beard. He wears false whiskers for the Parade each year. No reason he'd be wearing them this time of year."

"Maybe he was wearing whiskers as a disguise."

"Really? Disguised as Santa? Like nobody would notice?"

"Jeff is co-owner of the flower shop where Mycroft was killed. That puts him on the scene."

"If he was gonna kill somebody he wouldn't do it at his own shop. Besides, Ollie Micherson gave him an alibi."

"Oh, that's right." Evers thought a moment. "What about one of the Amish. All the married ones have beards. Some have white hair."

"Not many are fat. Healthy eaters, hard workers. They tend to be slender."

"But some are."

"What would be the motive? Amish don't rob people."

"You're right, they don't mingle much with Englanders. That's what they call us, y'know."

"Reverse bigotry," opined Hitzer. There was an unacknowledged tension between the two differing communities. "They don't approve of our lifestyle anymore than we approve of their buggies and old-fashion ways."

"That might be a motive. They don't approve of gays."

"Doubt that's it. The Amish are pretty much live-and-let-live people. Non violent."

Evers Gochnauer shrugged. "It was just a thought."

"So the Chief is convinced it was Fatty?" pressed Petie Hitzer.

"Well, Fatty *has* been trying to promote his ancestor as a town founder. And it's well-known that the Jinks don't like the Madisons or Caruthers getting all the credit."

"Bad blood, you're saying."

"As good a motive as any."

~ ~ ~

"Do you think we'll be safe?" asked Maddy as she stared from the upstairs window at the black sports utility vehicle parked across the street. A similar BMW X5 was parked in the alleyway on the other side of the back fence. Iron Fist Enterprises on the job.

"Of course, dear. These men are professionals. I'm told they acted as bodyguards for Vanilla Ice when he did a concert in Indy last year."

Maddy looked surprised. "Since when did you become fan of a rap music?"

"I'm just saying Jim checked out their credentials. They also bodyguard David Letterman when he comes to town. He's from Indy, y'know."

"I miss his Late Night television show," sighed Maddy. "He has such a cute gapped-tooth smile."

"Don't worry about those bodyguards outside. This is just till the murderer is caught. Jim Purdue says he's about to make an arrest."

CHAPTER TWENTY-NINE

The False Arrest

"Come out with your hands up, Fatty!" shouted Deputy Pete Hitzer, service pistol drawn. He was backed up by Deputy Evers Gochnauer, who had taken up a well-shielded position behind his police cruiser, pump shotgun peeking over the car's fender. This was as close to a SWAT team as the Caruthers Corners Police Department budget could fund.

"What's going on?" came a voice from the other side of the door. The farmhouse was owned by Clara Eloise Johnson, but she shared it with her two sons, Cromwell and Clovis.

Cromwell Thaddeus Johnson – better known as Fatty – had moved back in with his mom after his wife divorced him, taking their house on Jinks Lane in the settlement.

"Got a warrant for your arrest, Fatty," explained Deputy Hitzer. "Don't give us no trouble, you hear?"

"Arrest me for what?"

"Murder of Beau Madison's brother," said the deputy. "We got a witness."

"Heck you say. Can't be a witness to something I didn't do."

"He saw you at the scene of the crime when Mycroft Madison was murdered last Tuesday morning."

"I wasn't anywhere near the murder scene."

"Better come out before things go bad," shouted

Deputy Gochnauer from the safety of his police cruiser. He ratcheted back his 12-guage shotgun as a warning.

"Hold up there, Evers," said his partner. "No need to escalate this."

"Yeah, let's keep this civil," called Fatty. "You boys have known me all your lives. I'm not a murderer."

"Says you," growled Deputy Gochnauer.

"Says me," replied the voice behind the door. "I got me an iron-clad alibi. Mycroft Madison was killed on Tuesday. I took my mom to the doctor that morning. Check with Doc Medford."

~ ~ ~

"You sure about that?" said Chief Purdue, phone pressed against his ear. This didn't sound good. He had Fatty Johnson locked up in a holding cell. The mayor wasn't going to be happy if this led to a wrongful arrest lawsuit.

Fatty Johnson was a litigious man. He remembered when Fatty had sued the town for falling off a float during the Christmas Parade. The insurance firm had settled for a modest sum, just enough to whet Fatty's appetite to try again.

"Absolutely sure," replied Franklin D. Medford, MD. "I remember I was examining Fatty's mother when I got the call to go to the murder scene. Fatty was awfully mad that I cut her exam short."

"How is Fatty's mom?"

"Just as fat as Fatty. I'm surprised she hasn't had a stroke. The term we use is morbid obesity."

"I thought she had diabetes."

"She does. The whole family's got it. Fatty and his mother are on insulin. Fatty's brother takes metformin.

Wouldn't be so bad if they'd go on a diet and lose a little weight."

"Well, thanks, Doc. I've gotta go eat crow. That's *my* new diet."

"Good luck. I suspect you'll see Fatty in court."

"Yeah, no doubt. Greedy tub of lard."

"How did you make a mistaken identity?"

"Got a witness. But I should've known the guy was lying when he said the murderer was Santa Claus."

"Don't tell me you still believe in Santa," chuckled Doc Medford.

"Next thing you know I'll be arresting the Easter Bunny."

~ ~ ~

Mark the Shark moved fast. He gave Fatty Johnson a $2,000 check and had him sign a waiver, relieving the town and the police department of any claims for false arrest. Being quite greedy, Fatty signed on the spot. Two grand in the hand was worth more than a shaky lawsuit in the bush. Now he could pay Jeb Crackleton back that loan.

Chief Jim Purdue took his dressing down with grace, knowing the two grand would come out of his next year's raise. Oh well. That's what you get for trusting the word of a devious little con man like Eggie Ettelman. No plea bargaining for him. The lying rat could rot in the federal pen at Terre Haute the rest of his life for all Jim Purdue cared.

As for the murder of Mycroft Madison, and the attempts on Beau Madison and his family, Chief Purdue was back to square one. Who had it in for the Madisons?

PART THREE

The Gold

"You are damaged and broken and unhinged. But so
are shooting stars and comets."
- Nikita Gill, *Shooting Stars and Comets*

Chapter Thirty

Granny Again

Winston Gaylord Lockwood knocked on the door of the shack across from Crossroads Mercantile & Gas. When Granny Crackleton came to the door, opening it only enough to peek out with one rheumy eye, Lockwood quickly introduced himself as the writer who'd been hired to do a book on Ferdinand Aloysius Jinks. "I wonder if you might have a few minutes to talk?" he continued. "Being the oldest woman in the county I suspect you might have some tales to pass on."

"About Ferdie Jinks? He was before my time. How old do you think I am, sonny boy?"

"I heard you know all the dirt about the town's founding families."

"But you want the dirt on the Jinkses – right?"

He smiled. "Whatever you can tell me."

She opened the door to invite him inside. "Ferdinand Jinks died of spontaneous combustion, my mama told me. She knew all three of his sons. Ferdinand Junior was a pistol, always getting in trouble."

"Like what?" Lockwood settled into a worn easy chair.

"Junior burned down the old schoolhouse. Classes were disrupted for three months till a temporary structure could be built. He was a hero among the school children."

"Why did he do that?"

"I hadn't been born, so all I know is what my mama told me. She said the schoolmaster did not promote Junior to the sixth grade, so the boy burned down the schoolhouse in revenge. His daddy had to pay for a new building."

"You say Ferdinand Jinks died from ... spontaneous combustion? But according to Martin J. Caruthers' history book, the old man died from smoking in bed – a common house fire."

"I wouldn't believe a word any Caruthers has to say. Serpent tongues, all of them. My mama told me that story. And the one about the Jinks treasure. And about Junior burning down the schoolhouse. And the story about –"

Lockwood raised a hand. "Hold on, ma'am. What's this about a treasure?"

"Never mind, that's an old story."

"Tell me more."

"My mama said Ferdie Jinks brought a wagonload of gold with him when he headed west. Sorta like carrying coals to Newcastle, bringing gold bullion westward. But his father had been a successful importer back in Boston. Thought gold was the best way to transport his wealth when he decided to relocate to Chicago. Back then it was still known as Fort Dearborne. The Indians called it *Chicagou*, a word for the garlic that grew in the area."

"Yes, yes, but what about the gold?"

"My mama said the weight of the gold was what caused the wagon wheel to break. Other than that, there wouldn't be a Caruthers Corners. That's why

Fatty thinks the Jinks family deserves better recognition."

"What happened to the gold?"

"Now that's the mystery. Mama said ol' Ferdie hid it, nobody knows where. When I was a little girl, we children used to hunt for the treasure. Never did find anything."

~ ~ ~

That day a ten-foot snake escaped from Haney Bros. Circus and Petting Zoo, the exotic animal refuge just back of Bill Bentley's farm. Freddie Madison organized his fire department volunteers to go on a search for the missing reptile. The Burmese Python (*Python bivittatus*) is one of the five largest species of snakes in the world, known to attain a length up to eighteen feet. A dark-colored snake with brown blotches bordered in black, it's hard to spot among foliage.

Pia – as the snake is affectionately known to the school kids who visit the zoo – slipped through a crack in her cage, making off in search of mice or chipmunks for a midnight snack. Domestic farm cats were at risk too.

Being that pythons are fond of water, Big Bill Haney suspected she might head toward the Wabash, a few miles to the northwest. The firemen spread out, doing a ground search, walking about three feet apart. With only ten men, they had to cover the landscape in a careful grid pattern. Fortunately, most of it was pastureland or unplanted watermelon fields. Not many places for a large heavy-bodied nonvenomous constrictor snake to hide.

They found Pia near the river, relaxing in a butternut tree. Based on the bulge in her midsection, she had recently enjoyed an *al fresco* meal of woodrat or badger. She offered no objections to returning home to her comfortable habitat at the zoo.

While looking for the python, the searchers had stumbled across a small building hidden in a copse of trees near the old Ferdinand Jinks homestead. Of fairly new construction -- plywood walls and tin roofing -- it looked more like a hunting blind than a hobo's hut, although there were clear signs of recent habitation. Two cots were neatly made; clothing folded and stored in cardboard boxes; canned goods on a shelf.

One of Freddie's firemen found a wallet with a driver's license in the name of El Aloysius Crackleton. Were Jeb's twins living out here in an illegal domicile on Boyd Aitken's land?

Freddie made a note to tell Boyd about it next time he bumped into the watermelon farmer. Squatting out here in the bush was odd behavior even for a Crackleton.

What were the boys up to? Not hunting. There wasn't any decent game out here, other than the small vermin that a python found tasty.

The small shack's single window faced the stone house where the Jinks family had settled when the wagon train broke down hereabouts. Were the boys keeping watch on the abandoned stone house? If so, for what purpose?

But Freddie Madison didn't have time to puzzle over that. It would take all ten men and a panel truck to get Pia back to the Haney Bros. Circus and Petting Zoo.

CHAPTER THIRTY-ONE

The Skeleton Man

Cookie Bentley phoned Maddy that afternoon. "I think I know the identity of our skeleton man," she said excitedly.

"Really? How did you find that out?"

"You know I've been collecting local genealogy charts for the past ten years. Last year I put them all up on Ancestors.com. The initials on that ring Dr. Oakland found were ACEJ. So I took all the families with surnames beginning with J and looked for ancestors with those initials. I found only one – Aloysius Cromwell Edward Jinks."

"Who was he? Other than a descendant of one of the town founders."

"He was Ferdinand Jinks's youngest son. Unfortunately, I don't have anything about him but name and date of birth. December 1872."

"December – that explains the ruby in the ring," said Maddy.

"Apparently, he was a late-in-life child. Ferdie Jinks would've been 70 at the time. She was 42."

"Late in life or a friendly neighbor?"

"Ferdie Jinks remarried after his first wife got scalped by Indians. He married a much younger woman. Not always a good idea."

"Hey," protested Maddy. "My husband Beau was a late-in-life baby. His father was 75 when he was born.

That's a testament to the virility of the men in the Madison family."

"Go ahead and brag," Lizzie rolled her eyes. She and Edgar had slept in separate bedrooms for years now.

Bootsie said, "Is there anything in *A History of Caruthers Corners and Surrounding Environs* about this Aloysius Cromwell Edward Jinks?" She was referring to the one-sided account by the grandson of the man the town was named after.

"Not even a mention of the boy's name," replied Cookie. "But you know how Martin J. Caruthers tried to leave the Jinks family out of his history book. The Jinks descendants are angry over that slight to this very day."

~ ~ ~

"Maybe Granny Crackleton knows something about this missing Jinks boy," suggested Lizzie. She'd felt certain there was more the old woman wasn't telling when she visited her recently.

"Maybe," agreed Cookie. "But I don't relish a visit to Cuckoo Crossing to ask her. Those people up there are weird."

"Ah, what's an extra toe or two?" teased Maddy. "I'll go with you this time."

"Me too," volunteered Aggie. The girl had been fascinated by her earlier trip with Lizzie. She'd seen a man with three ears lingering across the street at the general store. The extra auricle looked like something applied by a Hollywood makeup man for a horror movie.

"I wanna go too," begged N'yen. His curiosity

sparked by Aggie's exaggerated tales about Crackleton Crossing. She made it sound like a visit to a carnival sideshow.

"Now children –" Maddy began a negative reply. Her daughter Tilly hadn't been pleased with Liz taking Aggie to visit Granny Crackleton last time.

"Please, please, please," wheedled N'yen.

"Let's all go," suggested Bootsie, always the fearless one. "There's safety in numbers."

"You make it sound like an episode of *The Walking Dead*," laughed Lizzie. A few years earlier she would have said *Night of the Living Dead*, but zombies and vampires had taken over the cable television channels. "It's perfectly safe up there. Jebediah Crackleton runs Cuckoo Crossing with an iron fist. You'd think he was its mayor."

"– or dictator," said Cookie. "Ever since he won that Powerball money he's been in total control."

"Money equals power," observed Maddy. They were in the hobby room at the Hoosier State Senior Recreational Center, working to complete the Community Quilt for Willamina Haney.

"Jim says Jeb Crackleton's a loan shark," confided Bootsie. "Doling out small amounts of money to people at usurious interest rates. But Jim can't prove it. Nobody will say a thing against Jeb."

"Is he really seven foot tall?" asked N'yen. He had been listening to Aggie's tales about her visit to Crossroads Mercantile & Gas.

"Actually, six-foot-eleven. Nearly seven feet," said Cookie. "Officially the tallest guy in the state."

"How do you know his exact height?" asked Bootsie.

"The Baltimore Geographical Society did a study of

Crackleton Crossing a few years back. The Historical Society has a copy of the report. The folks up there tried to burn all the copies, but I salvaged one."

"It was that bad?"

"The report recorded all kinds of statistics: extremisms in height, weight, digits, and such. Jeb Crackleton was the tallest member of the community; his son Willard the shortest at four-foot-two."

"Willard – is he the one they call Dub?" asked Maddy.

"That's him. Short for W. He manages the general store."

"Oh," said Aggie. "He's the little man with six fingers on one hand."

Cookie nodded. "The Baltimore report listed 39 physical abnormalities among the community. They range from extra digits to a guy with three ears."

"I saw him," bragged Aggie. "He was standing outside the general store."

"I heard there's a guy with a foot coming out of his stomach," said Bootsie.

"Yes, that's true. He has what's known as a parasitic twin. *Fetus in fetu* is the proper term. That's when one fetus envelops the other during conception. That enveloped twin grows inside, or sometimes partially inside, its brother. According to the Baltimore Geographical Society, there are fewer than 90 cases of *fetus in fetu* recorded in all medical literature. There are two in Caruthers Crossing."

"Two?"

"The foot-out-of-the-stomach guy and another fellow who has two sets of teeth, a leftover from a twin brother who didn't quite develop."

"Wow. That's like something out of science fiction," said Aggie. Eyes wide.

"That's also the process that causes conjoined twins," N'yen spoke up. "What's sometimes called Siamese twins ... although that Far Eastern King-and-I country has nothing to do with the medical condition." He was always sounding like a know-it-all. But he usually did know it all.

"All this comes from inbreeding?" asked Bootsie. As a teenager she'd once dated a distant cousin before they realized the familial connection. Close enough to scare her. That was before she met Jim.

"Nobody's entirely sure," shrugged Cookie. "But likely so in the case of Cuckoo Crossing."

Lizzie said, "In addition to Dub, Jeb Crackleton has two 'normal' sons – at least in terms of size and looks."

"I always forget about them," said Bootsie. "El and Vis, they're twins."

"So was Elvis," Cookie pointed out. "But his brother Jesse died at childbirth."

"They may look normal," said Maddy, "but I don't think those boys are right in the head. They seem to be living in a parallel universe to the rest of us."

"True," agreed Cookie. "El and Vis *are* pretty creepy."

"Granny Crackleton seems normal," observed Lizzie, "although a mite garrulous."

"She has a right to be cranky," said Maddy. "Keep in mind she's nearly 98 years old."

"How much is that in dog years," joked Aggie. She was petting her dog Tige.

"About fourteen," N'yen calculated, dividing the old woman's age by seven.

"No matter how you look at it," commented Cookie, "she's older than dirt."

Maddy began packing up her fabric scraps. "Okay,

let's go ask Granny about Aloysius Cromwell Edward Jinks before she drops dead from old age."

"What about your bodyguard?" asked Bootsie. He was sitting in his SUV in the senior center parking lot at this very minute, keeping watch.

"He can follow us," laughed Maddy. "Going to Cuckoo Crossing, we may need one."

CHAPTER THIRTY-TWO

Return to Cuckoo Crossing

Maddy parked her Toyota Sequoia in a slot to the side of Crossroads Mercantile & Gas. Granny Crackleton lived directly across the street in a house owned by her son Jeb. It was a tumbledown affair, unpainted wood and sagging porch, the yard as bare of grass as the Gobi Desert.

The black BMW parked beside them, Maddy's bodyguard at the ready. He was a beefy guy named Rex Blouderman, although his boss referred to him as X-3. The passengers in the blue Toyota more or less ignored him.

"Who's going in?" asked Maddy.

"I don't mind doing it again," said Lizzie, fluffing her red hair and checking her lipstick in the side mirror. She slipped out of the vehicle and pranced toward the shack.

"Wait for me!" shouted Aggie, scrambling out behind her.

"Me too!" declared N'yen.

"I suppose I'll go too," sighed Cookie. "After all, I'm supposed to be the expert on local genealogy."

The entourage was greeted by the front door swinging open before anyone could knock. "Ah, you're back," Sarah Celine Crackleton recognized Lizzie. "Come on inside, you an' your friends."

"We had another question," said Lizzie.

"Yes, a question about one of Ferdinand Jinks's sons," added Cookie.

Granny Crackleton turned her attention to the mousy brown-haired woman in glasses. "You're that History Society woman, ain't you? Seen your picture on a poster. You're the one showing off the falling star."

"The Madison Meteorite," Cookie nodded.

"Madison Meteorite is it now?"

"Yes," answered Cookie. "That was Beau Madison's condition for donating the meteorite to the Historical Society. It's been in the family since his father found it back in 1896."

"I know the story well. Heard it from Beauregard Madison III himself. He was an old man who liked entertaining young girls with his adventures. He told me all about finding that falling star."

"Did he mention the name of Aloysius Cromwell Edward Jinks?" interjected Lizzie.

"Ace he was called. Ferdie Jinks's youngest son. Ol' Beauregard felt badly about the boy. Maybe if he'd gone for help Ace coulda been saved. Everybody thought the boy had run away from home. Beau didn't mention his fate for over half a century. By then, nobody believed his stories. But I did. Beauregard wouldn't-a lied about something like that."

"What *did* happen to ... uh, Ace?" Lizzie tried to put it delicately.

"He got hit by that falling star. Thought I told you that last time you was here."

"You didn't say who it was."

"Ace. It was Ace. Nobody ever saw him after that, so Beau was likely telling the straight-up truth."

Cookie said, "A few days ago we found a skeleton beneath the rubble of the old stone silo. There was a ring inscribed ACEJ – for Aloysius Cromwell Edward Jinks."

"That proves it," the old woman crowed. "Beauregard said he didn't know if the boy survived the collapse of the silo or not. Said he hoped the boy had crawled away an' simply disappeared. But looks like you just proved he was kilt by that falling star."

Aggie looked pained. "So my grandfather didn't tell anybody Ace had been in the silo and his family thought he'd run away from home?"

The old woman nodded. "That's about the sum of it, missy."

"That's why there was no mention of him in the old newspapers," observed Cookie. "There would be no report of a young man leaving home to seek his fortune."

~ ~ ~

Maddy and Bootsie stepped into the general store. Dub Crackleton sat on his high stool behind the counter, an antiquated cash register within easy reach. *National* was embossed in brass letters on its side. Dub could have passed for a Harry Potter house elf. He was afflicted with proportionate dwarfism, the result of a growth hormone deficiency associated with the anterior pituitary. The result of a genetic mutation. He preferred being called "a small person."

The store was cluttered. Shelves crisscrossed the square room displaying canned goods and cellophaned snack cakes and 10W30 motor oil and packets of slim jims. Drink coolers lined the entire wall on the right side.

A katydid stick figure occupied a table on the left side of the store – Jebediah Crackleton, judging from his elongated frame. He glared at them from afar, a threatening figure.

"Help you ladies?" Dub called out in his high-pitched voice. Like his father, he recognized Maddy as the former mayor's wife; the other as the police chief's wife. Highfalutin customers for this simple country outpost.

Bootsie spoke up, "Yes, thank you. Six Cokes, please."

"Seven," Maddy corrected her, mindful of the bodyguard outside in the black SUV. May as well be polite to ol' X-3, even if he was like an unwanted chaperone at a prom dance.

The tiny man behind the counter grunted, "You'll find 'em in that first cooler over there. That'll be a dollar each – seven bucks in all." Then, ignoring them, he went back to reading his week-old newspaper. His face reflected a dark scowl, as if like his father he resented their presence.

Nestled inside the red cooler they found green-tinted bottles of Coca-Cola, sweaty and cold to the touch. Maddy took four and Bootsie took three, leaving $7 on the counter in wrinkled dollar bills.

As they approached the door, a voice from corner table stopped them. "Hear your husband arrested my cousin Fatty Johnson."

Bootsie turned to face Jeb Crackleton. "He's out now. Apparently it was a case of mistaken identity."

"Yeah, you got the wrong man. His baby brother's a more likely candidate to be killing off Madisons."

"And why is that?" responded Maddy.

"Boy's got a screw loose. Everybody knows that. Fatty's always complaining how the Madisons and Caruthers hogged all the glory, cutting out Ferdinand Jinks. But Clovis is the one what takes it seriously. He's a real wackjob, even by Crackleton standards."

"Why are you telling us this?" asked Bootsie.

"Cause Fatty owes me money. He can't pay it back if he's locked up in jail. I'd rather you get the right guy – even if it is a relative – than interfere with my payments."

"I'll pass your message on to my husband," said Bootsie. Careful not to overpromise. The tall man was kinda scary, like that Jack Skellington character in *The Nightmare Before Christmas*.

Chapter Thirty-Three

Waylaid on Highway 101

On the way back to town, Maddy's car had a blowout. The big Sequoia was crossing the Highway 101 bridge over the Wabash when she heard a popping sound and the vehicle lurched to the right, heading straight toward the bridge abutment. It was all she could do to wrestle the vehicle to a stop, inches from the concrete guardrail. The occupants were screaming like riders on the Steel Hawg coaster at Indiana Beach. Fortunately, everybody was wearing a seat belt.

Behind them the black SUV swerved to avoid a collision. X-3 was a skillful wheelman, having once been a pace car driver in the Indy 500. His bumper stopped inches from Maddy's taillight.

"What the heck?" Maddy exclaimed, sitting there behind the wheel, shaking.

"Grammy, you almost wrecked," chided Aggie.

"We blew a tire," N'yen said calmly from the backseat. "Right front, I think."

"What caused that?" wondered Lizzie, fluffing her hair back in place. She'd paid $45 to have her hair done yesterday at the Helen of Troy Spa and Beauty Salon in Burpyville and wasn't happy to have it mussed up.

"Maybe a nail on the road," speculated Cookie. "It happens."

Just then came a tapping at the driver's window – Agent X-3. Maddy pressed the button to lower the glass.

"That was close," she told him with a sheepish grin. "Almost hit the side of the bridge. Solid concrete, that would have hurt."

"Yes ma'am. Your right front tire went out."

"Told you," muttered N'yen from the backseat.

"A booby trap by all appearances," continued X-3, the erstwhile Rex Blouderman. "Somebody put boards with nails in them across this lane of the highway."

"You're saying someone deliberately tried to wreck us?" exclaimed Bootsie. As a policeman's wife, she was immediately on the case. Pulling out her Samsung phone, she dialed the Caruthers Corners Police Department. As you might expect, the number was on her speed dial.

"Apparently so," replied X-3. "The boards look like something an Indian fakir might lay on, nails pointing upward." His voice sounded full of concern, but it was more his worry that Drake Hammer would ream him out for nearly losing his charges. Definitely a no-no in the personal security business.

Maddy and the others stepped out of the Sequoia to inspect the object that caused them to nearly wreck. Three 2" x 4" x 24" boards were scattered across the pavement, each looking like a strip of metal lawn with nails for grass. A miracle the car's tires had only hit one of the boards, taking out the right Firestone LE2 All-Season Radial. The cost was $183.99 each at Flynn's Texaco, not including mounting. There went this month's eating-out budget.

By now Bootsie had her hubby on the line, reporting the sabotage on the Highway 101 bridge.

"That's the same bridge where somebody tried to

drop a cement block on Beau's head," Jim Purdue observed. "Maybe our perp lives near there. Seems to be a convenient place for his murder attempts."

"Nothing out this way but farmland. Crackleton Crossing is the closest cluster of houses."

"This is – what? – the sixth assault on a Madison."

"More than just Madisons. This one would have taken out me and Lizzie and Cookie too!" his wife rejoined.

"The perp seems to be escalating."

"Will you call Buddy Flynn to come fix the tire for Maddy? She's got Triple-A."

"Already had the dispatcher do that. And Petie Hitzer's on his way to the scene. Should be there within ten or fifteen minutes. He was already out that way, checking out a complaint about somebody stealing building supplies at a construction site. That new home Fat Karl Schaeffer's building on Watermelon Road."

"Not boards and nails by any chance?"

"Oh, I see what you mean. I'll have Petie see if he can make any connection."

~ ~ ~

Daniel Sokolowski had been doing a little research. That design on the ring found in the ruins of the old silo had been tugging at the corner of his mind, some significance that he couldn't quite place.

With French jewelry and Swiss watches, you usually find both maker's marks and hallmarks. But many countries – including the US – do not have a hallmarking system. Although reputable firms often mark their fine jewelry, registering these marks isn't required. So there's no good place to research the identity of a signature or mark.

Rings were once considered sacred objects. Goddesses and gods wore rings. Babylonian mythology tells stories about the rings of Shamas and Marduk.

Sometimes rings were functional. Archers' thumb rings were worn by the Chinese, Turks, and Persians. They covered the thumb of the left hand to protect it from injury by the bowstring when shooting an arrow.

Thimble rings were the same, utilitarian for sewers.

In the sixteenth century it was customary to assign rings to certain fingers according to the wearer's profession or personality:

- The thumb for doctors.
- The index finger for merchants.
- The middle finger for fools.
- The annular finger for students.
- The auricular finger for lovers.

Chief Purdue had asked Dan to clean the dirt-encrusted ring. That's when the antiques dealer discovered that the "design" circling the band was actually script. When examined under a jeweler's loupe, the weatherworn message read: *The foundation of my home is golden.* Followed by the date 1872.

Yes, despite the ruby gemstone, this was a form of posy ring.

Posy rings derive their name from the French word "poésie," meaning poem. Typically, these finger rings were engraved with rhyming messages of one or two lines. The inscriptions often declared friendship, professed loyalty, offered a religious thought, or spoke of love.

These rings were popular from the latter half of the

Middle Ages through the Victorian Era. Samuel Pepys mentioned them in his diary; Shakespeare referred to them in *Hamlet* and *The Merchant of Venice*. The Victoria & Albert Museum in London houses the largest collection of posy rings in the world.

Message were usually personal and unique. Among the rhymes and ruminations were such lines as *"In thee my choyce I doe reioyce"* ... *"Bee firme in faith"* ... *"Content is a treasure"* ... *"A vertuous wife preseurueth life"* ... and *"As gold is pure, so love is sure."*

Early on, the phrases were written in Latin, Old French or Old English. Until about 1350 the lettering was done in a script with rounded Lombardic capital letters. Later examples used Gothic script.

Posy rings from the medieval period had the words engraved around the outside of the band, while with later examples the lettering was often secreted inside.

The rings were commonly gold bands, ofttimes plain except for the inscribed words, although sometimes decorative with designs or pictographs. Rarely was there a gemstone.

A close examination of the ring from the ruins of the silo revealed that it was 14-karat gold, featured a genuine ruby, and the outer band incorporated a folksy homily. 1872 was probably the date it was made. The ACEJ initials inside the ring were either those of the owner or that of the goldsmith who crafted it. Owner, he thought, given the period of the late 1800s in frontier America.

Those Quilters Club gals would find this very interesting, Daniel Sokolowski told himself. Another clue in a century-old murder mystery.

Chapter Thirty-Four

Considering a New Suspect

Beau Madison's own bodyguard – X-2, as Jerry Walberg liked to be called – drove him down to Caruthers Corners Savings and Loan where he extracted his grandfather's diary from the safe deposit box. Its yellowed pages were bound between brown leather covers. The words MY LIFE STORY were burnt into the leather, a technique known as pyrography. Beau had owned a woodburning kit when he was a kid, so he understood the process of etching letters onto wood or leather with the tip of a hot pen.

Maddy had called him on her iPhone, forewarning about the mishap on the Highway 101 bridge. She also mentioned that Granny Crackleton confirmed that Ferdinand Jinks's youngest son had been killed by the meteorite which struck the stone silo in 1896.

"Well, you ferreted it out," Beau told her. "That's the family secret. My father left Ace Jinks to die there in the rubble of the silo."

"Pooh Bear, you may as well accept the past for what it is. You can't hide the truth."

"Yeah, guess you're right."

With nothing more to keep secret, Beau reluctantly decided to turn Beau Three's diary over to the Historical Society. Cookie was overjoyed with the news, her near-death experience on the Highway 101 Bridge now forgotten.

~ ~ ~

His wife's 2015 Toyota Sequoia was parked in the driveway when he got back to their Victorian home on Melon Pickers Row. The other Iron Fist SUV was parked behind her, so X-2 edged his own vehicle to the curb in front of the house. Other cars lined the street.

Beau was upset that this deranged killer had made an attempt on his wife and her friends. And with two children in the car. Did this monster have no conscience?

"Hon, are you all right?" he called as he rushed into the house. A crowd had gathered in the living room. Not only the members of the Quilters Club, but husbands as well.

"I'm fine, Pooh Bear," Maddy greeted him. "We all are. But it was scary for a moment there on the bridge."

Just then Mark the Shark arrived, accompanied by his own bodyguard – X-1 or X-4, it wasn't clear which. No one other than Aggie and N'yen were impressed by these Dashiell Hammett-like designations. Hammett had co-created a comic strip with artist Alex Raymond titled *Secret Agent X-9*. Aggie had read the paperback collection in the school library and found it exciting.

"Jim, we've got to stop this madman," the mayor said to his police chief.

"That's f'sure," the lawman nodded his bald head. "Wish my witness had proved more reliable."

"He said the man who killed Mycroft looked like Santa Claus," Maddy pointed out. "That's what made you go after Fatty Johnson?"

"Yeah, but he had an alibi."

"What's your point?" asked her son-in-law. Looking more like a worried husband than a high-powered lawyer or popular mayor.

"Yeah," repeated the police chief.

"When we were in Cuckoo Crossing earlier today, Jeb Crackleton told us you were looking at the wrong guy," Maddy explained. "He said you should be checking out Fatty's brother Clovis."

"Clovis?" laughed Ben Bentley. "He hasn't got the brains God gave a billy goat. No way he could be pulling off a series of murders."

"Maybe that's the clue," offered Aggie. "He *hasn't* pulled them off, other than Uncle Mikey's. The rest have been fizzles: Uncle Freddie spotted the bomb under the fire truck; Uncle Billy managed to stop his car; that cement block missed Grampy's head; that shot missed my Mom; those nails didn't wreck Grammy's car."

"Yeah," N'yen seconded his cousin. "That's not much of a success record."

"See your point," Jim Purdue said, screwing up his mouth in thought. "Clovis does favor Santa Claus, especially after he grew that white beard last year. Wanted to look like his big brother, he said."

"But why would Clovis have it in for the Madison family?" asked Edgar Ridenour. "You folks never done anything to him."

"Jeb had a theory," said Maddy. "Clovis in his simple-minded way is trying to support his brother. Fatty started that Ferdinand Aloysius Jinks Heritage Society as a means of honoring his ancestor. Clovis is just carrying the resentment towards the Caruthers and Madisons to an extreme."

"That boy does worship his brother. He'd do

anything to please him," observed Ben Bentley.

"Boy?" snorted Edgar Ridenour. "He's got to be forty years old."

"He's still a boy in his feeble mind," his wife reminded him. She had always been creeped out by Fatty Johnson and his younger brother. Something was "off" about both of them.

"You will have to get some firm evidence," the mayor said to the police chief. "I don't want to have to buy off Clovis on a false-arrest claim too."

"Let me round him up," nodded Chief Jim Purdue. "That simpleton might just confess to the whole thing before I read him his rights."

~ ~ ~

Clovis Augustus Johnson sat at the counter of Cozy Café, slurping at a tall chocolate milk. That went well with his toasted cheese sandwich. His mom made great toasted cheese sandwiches, grilling them with butter in a cast-iron frying pan. She hadn't been home when he and his brother Fatty got back from Burpyville. They had been looking at a sculpture that was for sale, the likeness of some former statesman who might pass as Ferdinand Aloysius Jinks.

Clara Johnson usually had lunch waiting for her boys, but today the kitchen table was bare, no sign of her. So Fatty had suggested they eat at Cozy Café. Clovis was hesitant until his brother promised he could have chocolate milk. He had a taste for chocolate.

Fatty slouched next to his brother at the counter, munching on his toasted cheese. Maisie Walters refilled his coffee cup. Even though she now owned the restaurant, she still worked shifts as a waitress. Old habits.

"Where's mom?" Clovis asked between sips of chocolate milk. "She hasn't left us, has she?"

"Don't be daft," grumbled Fatty. "She's probably shopping at the Food Lion. Didn't expect us back from Burpyville this early."

"Are you gonna buy that shiny old statue?" Clovis asked.

"Maybe, if I can pass it off as Ferdinand Jinks. It's cheaper than that statue of Jefferson Davis I was considering. Or getting one made in Chicago."

"If this statue isn't really ol' Ferdie, who is it?"

Fatty shrugged, hunching his pudgy shoulders. "A former US Congressman named Lincoln Dixon. He was born in Vernon, Indiana. Don't know why they had a statue of him over in Burpyville."

"Why they selling it?"

"The Park Commission is replacing it with a statue of James Dean. The actor was born in Marion, a town that's between Burpyville and Indianapolis."

"James Dean?"

"You know, Jimmy Dean, the actor in that movie *East of Eden*. We saw it last month on the American Movie Channel."

Clovis looked confused. "Jimmy Dean? I thought he made sausage."

"Just drink your chocolate milk."

Chapter Thirty-Five

Reading the Diary

The next day Maddy's husband drove up High Jinks Hill to the Historical Society to deliver his father's diary. The bodyguard followed him in the black SUV. Cookie could barely wait to examine the historic document. But when it came down to it, only the entry for November 17, 1896, held any interest. She read it out loud, moving her finger along the wavering lines of Beauregard Hollingsworth Madison III's handwritten scrawl:

In the early evening of Tuesday I spyed a shooting star. It was close to 7 of-the-clock. At first I heard a hissing sound and looked up into the heavens in time to sight a fireball heading toward earth. It struck the silo that stood in the center of my father's side pasture, causing the structure to collapse like a stack of children's building blocks. That caused a great clamor. My friend Ace had been at the top of the silo, tho I didn't see him amid the dust and scattered stones. My first thought was that he was a sissy, having run home out of fear. I was more intrigued by an indention in the earth made by the fallen star. There lay a blackened rock, seeming far too small to have caused all that damage. I picked it up and took it home, abandoning my search for a missing bovine we affectionately called Blue Belle. I never laid eyes on Ace again. I told few friends this tale, for fear of being blamed for my friend's disappearance or demise.

"There's your confirmation," Beau said to Cookie. "The Madison Meteorite *did* kill someone. Just as the legend had it."

"This will be great for the Historical Society's new exhibit. Newspapers across the country will pick up this story. One of the few people in history to be killed by a meteorite. I wonder if the Jinks descendants would let me put the bones on display. It would be one heckuva show."

"That seems somehow disrespectful," said Beau.

"Not at all. Think of it as a belated wake. After more than a century, Ace Jinks deserves to be laid out for a viewing."

"There's nothing left to view but a pile of bones," Beau argued.

"Churches in Europe put bones on display."

Beau drew the conversation to a close. "Those are sacred bones," he said sternly. "Priests and martyrs and the like. Ace Jinks was just a farm boy who found himself in the wrong place at the wrong time. He deserves a little belated respect."

~ ~ ~

"When Aunt Lizzie and I went to talk with Granny Crackleton she told us lots of stories about the old days," said Aggie. She was helping her Grammy with the dishes. Dinner had been roast beef with a delicious watermelon sauce.

"I've probably heard them all," laughed Maddy, scouring on a pan. "But only half are true, I suspect."

"She said Ferdinand Jinks burned up by spontaneous combustion. Disappeared in a bright flash. Is there such a thing?"

"That's an old wives tale. I doubt people burst into flames."

N'yen had been helping dry. "Actually spontaneous combustion is quite common. It happens with oily rags, charcoal, even hay."

"But people?" His grandmother was skeptical.

"That's technically called spontaneous human combustion, or SHC. It's the theory that people can ignite by internal means. However, current scientific consensus is that most cases involve external sources of ignition that were overlooked by investigators."

"So it's not real?" asked Aggie.

N'yen rolled his eyes. "Well, people *have* been known to burn up. The question is how."

"Granny Crackleton also told us about Ferdinand Jinks's son burning down the schoolhouse."

"I've heard that story too," laughed Maddy. "Don't get any ideas, you two. That would be a serious crime. Probably a life sentence at the state reformatory school."

N'yen said, "Really, Grammy. Do we look like arsonists?"

Aggie paused to think. "What about the lost treasure? Did you ever hear about that?"

Maddy blinked. "What lost treasure?"

"That old woman said Ferdinand Jinks had a wagon filled with gold," replied N'yen. "But the gold's never been found."

"That's a new one on me," said Maddy. "Are you sure that's what she said?"

Aggie nodded, her blonde hair bobbing. "Ask Aunt Lizzie or Aunt Cookie. They heard it too."

"I was there. I heard her say it," N'yen jumped in.

"Just because Sarah Crackleton told it doesn't make it true," said Maddy, putting away the last dish. "I think she makes up things to entertain visitors."

"Granny Crackleton had lots of stories. But mostly we talked about that boy getting killed by the meteorite. Ace, she called him."

"But she did tell us about the missing gold," N'yen insisted.

"Missing gold," smiled Maddy. We'll have to ask your Aunt Cookie about that farfetched fairy tale. Bet she'll say it's hogwash."

~ ~ ~

Winston Gaylord Lockwood was actually the pen name for a writer whose birth certificate identified him as Carl Bernstein. No, not the Watergate journalist. But if you had the same name as a newspaperman whose work had been called "maybe the single greatest reporting effort of all time," you'd use a pseudonym too. Didn't matter if you carried a copy of your birth certificate around in your pocket, nobody would believe you were really "that guy." They'd think you were a liar.

Fatty Johnson's check had bounced, so the idea of

writing a biography about an obscure old pioneer like Ferdinand Jinks was off the table. The tub of lard was a deadbeat. He could write his own book if he wanted one.

Nevertheless Carl couldn't help but ruminate on the interview he'd had with that old biddy, Sarah Celine Crackleton. Some said Granny Crackleton was a "witch woman," but Carl figured she was more senile than anything else. But that didn't make her wrong.

She had told him about a wagonload of gold bullion that had gone missing. Now *that* was interesting. If he could find that lost cache of gold, he'd never have to crank out another crappy book-for-hire. He didn't like being a for-rent hack.

Carl had once dreamed of writing the Great American Novel, but after three years locking himself in a cabin in the Colorado Rockies he'd only turned out 78 pages of drivel. That amounted to two pages a month. At some point you had to face up to the fact that you just didn't have it in you.

Granny Crackleton had told him local children used to dig up the yard around the old Ferdinand Jinks homeplace, a rundown stone building on a dirt road west of Never Ending Swamp. They thought the treasure was buried there. Might be worth a look-see, he thought to himself.

CHAPTER THIRTY-SIX

Stormtroopers

Rex Blouderman – that is, Agent X-3 – was blocking the walkway, preventing an elderly man from proceeding to the Madison's front door. "Sorry, Pops. Nobody goes in without a personal invitation."

"But I know Beauregard and Maddy," Daniel Sokolowski shouted, waving his cane. "Since when did Nazi *Sturmabteilung* have a say-so over their visitors?"

"Move it along. This house is off limits for the time being."

"*Al ta'atzben otti*! I need to see Maddy Madison," he shouted.

"No go, Pops."

Maddy appeared at the front door. "Daniel, what's going on?"

"This *ben kelev* is refusing me entrance."

"Rex, that's a friend of mine. It's okay for him to come in."

X-3 glowered. "If you say so, ma'am."

The burly man stood aside and Dan Sokolowski scurried toward his rescuer. "Maddy, I have something you will want to see," he huffed from the exertion of walking fast.

"What's is it?"

"The ring. As you know, Chief Purdue gave it to me to examine. And I have discovered something quite interesting."

He followed her into the living room. The earlier crowd had left, the police chief in search of Clovis Johnson, the others returning to their respective homes. Beau had accompanied Cookie Bentley over to the Historical Society to turn over his grandfather's leather-bound diary.

Aggie and young N'yen had stayed behind with their Grammy. They were using the boy's MacBook Pro to check messages on Facebook.

"Say hello to Mr. Sokolowski," instructed their grandmother.

Aggie glanced up long enough to say, "Hello, Mr. S." And N'yen muttered, "Hi."

"Hello, children. We are talking about the ring you found with the skeleton."

"Oh, that ring with the big red ruby," nodded Aggie. Her cousin ignored them, busy *liking* someone's Facebook page.

"That is the one," the old man acknowledged.

"We finally confirmed the owner of the ring," Maddy said as they settled onto the couch. On the coffee table was a pitcher of watermelon tea. She poured two cups as she talked. "ACEJ stands for Aloysius Cromwell Edward Jinks. He was the youngest son of ol' Ferdinand Jinks. Granny Crackleton confirmed it. Then my husband turned over his father's diary to the Historical Society. It documents everything – the sighting of the meteorite, it striking the stone silo, the disappearance of Ace Jinks, as the boy was called. All there in Beauregard Three's own handwriting."

"All very interesting. But why didn't the boy report his friend's death?"

"He wrote that he wasn't sure what happened to Ace. Thought he'd run home. When it became clear he was missing, it was too awkward to admit he'd abandoned his friend to his fate."

"The more curious question is why your husband kept his father's secret."

"Protecting the family name, I suppose. He didn't want to tarnish his father's image."

"Well, you've pretty much solved that mystery. All I can add is this: That ring you found is what's called a posy ring. That's a band with a message inscribed on it. Posy rings were quite popular in the Victorian Era, but you don't see them anymore. I didn't recognize what it was until I cleaned off the dirt."

"A message?"

"Well, a homily of some sort."

"What did it say?"

"Look," he produced the ring. "Around the outer band are the words: *The foundation of my home is golden.* A nice sentiment."

"Sounds like a fortune cookie," chuckled Maddy.

"Yes, a silly adage."

"Maybe it's more than that," Aggie spoke up. "What about the legend of the Jinks gold? Could this be a hint where to find it?"

~ ~ ~

"The Jinks gold?" said Dan Sokolowsi. "What's that?"" As an antique dealer who bought gold and silver jewelry and coins, the mention of precious metals always got his attention.

"Just an old wives tale," Maddy waved it away. "No basis in fact, according to my friend Cookie. As head of the Historical Society, she ought to know. I phoned her this morning."

"Granny Crackleton – that crazy old lady up in Cuckoo Crossing – told us about it," offered N'yen, looking up from his laptop. "Is she an old wife?"

"Probably as good an example as any," Dan Sokolowski chuckled. He was familiar with Granny Crackleton and her clan.

Aggie jumped in. "Granny said Ferdinand Jinks had a bunch of gold that went missing. People have been hunting for it ever since."

"Cookie says local kids used to play a game, hunting for the lost Jinks fortune," added Maddy. "That's about the size of it."

Dan Sokolowski rubbed his beard thoughtfully. "Even so, it might be worth the effort to take a look at the foundation of the Jinks homeplace. Just for the fun of it."

"Fun?" Maddy was surprised to hear the octogenarian speak of fun. It seemed out of character for such a dour individual. An immigrant from Eastern Europe – rumored to be a Holocaust survivor – the antiques dealer kept mostly to himself. Only in recent years had he become more sociable, friendly with her husband Beau, chatty with her granddaughter Aggie, even deigning to help the Quilters Club solve a few mysteries.

Dan Sokolowski shrugged, wincing from a touch of rheumatism. Then he smiled. "Well, it might be interesting to visit the homeplace built by one of the town's founders. Especially when Fatty Johnson's working so hard to get a statue of his forbearer erected in the town square."

"Did Fatty raise the money he was looking for?"

"I heard he borrowed it from Jebediah Crackleton. A bad decision. The man is a crook. Breaks all the usury laws. Fatty came to me looking to borrow $2,000. Apparently, that is what a used statue costs."

"Used?"

"He plans to pass off someone else's effigy as Ferdinand Jinks. A cost-saving move. But it seems wrong to have an imposter erected in the town square, don't you think?"

"Does Mark the Shark know about this scheme?"

"Dunno. When Fatty told me about it, I just laughed. It seemed so crazy. But there's Crackleton blood in Fatty's family tree. Witness his brother Clovis."

"Is Clovis crazy?" asked Aggie. She'd seen the roly-poly man about town, usually trailing behind his brother. He seemed ... well, childish.

"He's a little bit off," her grandmother said. "But not dangerous."

~ ~ ~

Police Chief Jim Purdue looked angry – and he was. The idea of Clovis Johnson being the killer made sense. He was a feeble-brained guy who worshipped his brother. And his brother revered their ancestor, Ferdinand Jinks. As a result Fatty hated the Caruthers and Madisons who had "stolen" ol' Ferdie's glory. It wasn't difficult to image Clovis getting rid of his brother's enemies.

Perhaps Clovis was doing this crime spree on his own, with the aim of pleasing Fatty.

What was that line by Henry II? *Who will rid me of*

this meddlesome priest? Upon hearing this complaint from their sovereign, four knights killed Thomas Beckett, the Archbishop of Canterbury.

Pleasing the boss.

"Let's go get him," said Chief Purdue. "Do we know where to find him?"

Deputy Pete Hitzer nodded. "He'll probably be at his mama's house."

"No shooting, He'll come quietly. Probably think we're taking him out for ice cream."

"Is the Mayor okay with this?" Petie was trying to be diplomatic. He knew the Chief had been reprimanded for arresting Fatty. After all, the man had an ironclad alibi.

"Don't worry. We're just bringing Clovis in for questioning. We'll find out if he has an alibi or not. I'm not making the same mistake twice."

"Still, we'd better be careful," said the deputy, fingering the butt of his service revolver. "Clovis is crazy as a stinkbug."

Chapter Thirty-Seven

Getting Squirrely

Clara Johnson blocked the doorway. "You can't come in here without a warrant," the prune-faced woman stated flatly. "You already tried to pin that murder on Cromwell. You're not gonna do that with Clovis."

"We just want to talk with your son Clovis. Nobody's making any accusations." Chief Purdue took off his cap and wiped his slick head with a handkerchief. It was warm for this early in the year. Global warming, no doubt.

"Clovis don't know nothing," the old woman stuck to her guns. "He ain't got the brains of a squirrel. That boy can't help you."

"Ask him come to the door, else I'll have to arrest you for obstructing justice."

"Oh, *pshaw*. Talk to him then, but I'm gonna hire me a lawyer. This amounts to police harassment."

"Thank you, Mrs. Johnson. I appreciate your cooperation."

There was a shuffling behind her and Clovis appeared, nudged along by his older brother. "Ah, I don't wanna talk to no police," whined Mrs. Johnson's younger son. "They scare me."

"It's okay, bro," coaxed Fatty. "Just get it over with. They talked with me and I'm back home with you. Nothing they can do to you either."

Looking at the two men standing side-by-side, it was like seeing döpplegangers. Clovis was shorter and a few years younger, but he was a mirror image of his brother.

"Clovis, where were you Tuesday morning before last?" asked the police chief.

"Dunno. Probably with Fatty."

"No, Fatty took your Mom to the doctor. Where were you?"

"Don't wanna say."

"C'mon, Clovis you've got to say. Tell him, Fatty."

The rotund man smacked his brother on the shoulder. "Tell 'em, Clovis. Me and Mom won't be mad."

The younger man hung his head. "I sneaked off for a chocolate milk at Cozy Café. Didn't figure anybody would know. Used my own money. I was a quarter short, but Miss Maisie said it was all right. I sure do love chocolate."

Chief Purdue looked at his deputy and shrugged. "That should be easy to confirm. Call Maisie Walters. See if she remembers serving Clovis on Tuesday week ago."

She did.

~ ~ ~

"D'you think I could be a bodyguard when I grow up?" N'yen asked the muscular man known as X-3. "I think it would be fun, protecting people from bad guys."

"Truth is, it's pretty dull," admitted Rex Blouderman. "Mostly, it's sitting around in my car, listening to music on the radio while rich folks eat dinner in a fancy restaurant or go shopping. There's hardly ever a physical confrontation, except when we're providing security for a celeb. Sometimes fans get out of hand and we have to give a show of force. But mostly it's just cooling our heels and looking tough."

"You are tough. I can tell," said the boy.

"Shucks, I used to be tough. I was pretty good at college football, but didn't make the Big Leagues. Had a good run with the Army in Afghanistan. Survived several firefights. Still got some shrapnel in my butt from an IED that went off near my armored Humvee."

"Wow! You're like a real-life Captain America."

"Hardly. I just try to protect the folks I work for. Like you."

"You don't work for me, d'you?"

"Sure I do. Somebody's paying me to protect your family."

"Hm, maybe we should have a secret signal, a way I can call you if I need help."

"Just say help. I'll be close by."

"But I might be in the house and you out in your car. I'd want to call you if a crazed ax murderer broke into the house."

"No way he'd get in with me out here and my partner in back."

"He might tunnel in from the house next door. Or parachute onto the roof from a plane."

"Doubt it. But here's my personal cell phone number." He handed N'yen a glossy card. "Just phone me anytime you need a little muscle."

"I've got a little muscle," said the boy. "If I phone you, it'll be because I need big muscles."

~ ~ ~

That afternoon Carl Bernstein purchased a shovel at Home Depot and drove out to the Jinks homestead. He parked his rental car in front of the dilapidated old stone building and walked a wide circle around the structure, taking its measure. If he were going to hide enough gold bullion to fill a covered wagon, where would be the ideal spot?

From what he'd learned about Ferdinand Jinks, the man wasn't one to let his treasure out of sight, so it was likely near his home. In the cellar. Buried in the yard. Secreted in an out building.

Unfortunately, near two centuries later any nearby barns, sheds, or chicken houses had long since disappeared. The stone homeplace was still standing – barely. Not a lot of options.

There were lots of holes in the yard that indicated recent digging, but he couldn't see any depressions in the surrounding pasture that might mark the settling of earth over something buried. No foundations for out buildings. And no sign of a hiding place in the large, dank cellar.

A total bust.

As he was coming up the cellar stairs, a shadow blocked his way. "Intruder!" it yelled in a high-pitched voice. "Get out of our house!" Then a baseball bat caught Carl Bernstein on the forehead, sending him tumbling backward, landing on the dirt cellar floor in a heap. Dead.

"Thanks for bringing a shovel," hissed the shadowy figure, breaking into a maniacal laugh. "It'll come in handy."

CHAPTER THIRTY-EIGHT

Preparing for the Exhibit

Cookie drove over to Burpyville to get some posters made. One poster announced the Madison Meteorite Exhibition. Another featured that salient passage from Beau's father's diary. And a third gave a definition from Dr. Archimedes Claypool's *Meteor Science and Celestial Observations:*

> "A meteorite is a piece of space debris such as a comet, asteroid, or meteoroid that enters the atmosphere and impacts the earth's surface."

Keep it simple, she thought.

Cookie had to be back at the Perricock Science & History Museum by 3 p.m. That's when the armored car company was scheduled to deliver the *Shooting Star Quilt 1898*, on loan from the Indiana State Museum. If she couldn't exhibit Ace Jinks's bones, the quilt would be a credible substitute. After all, it was a prime example of a Pictorial Quilt. And documented the meteorite's landing.

~ ~ ~

Pictorial Quilts by definition depict "clouds and skies, leaves and flowers, people, birds and animals, travel and transportation, and other popular motifs."

Perhaps the earliest known such quilt is *River of Life 1835* by Hannah Stockton Stiles. The 105" x 89" cotton-and-chintz bedcovering resides in the Fenimore

Art Museum in Cooperstown, New York. The piece is considered one of the greatest quilts of all time, the symbolic narrative equal to the finer paintings of the era.

Next came the Pictorial Quilts of Harriet Powers, an African American woman of Clarke County, Georgia. Powers had exhibited one of her quilts at the Athens Cotton Fair of 1886 where it captured the imagination of attendees. One observer wrote: "I have spent my whole life in the South, and am perfectly familiar with thirty patterns of quilts, but I had never seen an original design, and never a living creature portrayed in patchwork, until the year 1886 ... In one corner there hung a quilt which 'captured my eye' and after much difficulty I found the owner, a negro woman, who lives in the country on a little farm whereon she and her husband make a respectable living ... The scenes on the quilt were biblical and I was fascinated. I offered to buy it, but it was not for sale at any price."

Later, Harriet Powers sent word offering to sell the quilt because her family was facing hard times. The buyer wrote, "She arrived one afternoon in front of my door in an ox-cart with the precious burden in her lap encased in a clean flour sack, which was still further enveloped in a crocus sack. She offered it for ten dollars – but – I only had five to give." Mrs. Powers took it at the urging of her husband.

It's not known how many Pictorial Quilts Mrs. Powers made during her lifetime, but she mentioned in a letter making a Star Quilt and one of the Lord's Supper. Historians have compared her work to textiles of Dahomey, West Africa.

Mary Louise Madison's *Shooting Star Quilt 1898*

was much more documentarian in theme, recording the approach of a fiery meteorite. "Her style is bold," one art critic observed, "more akin to naïve art. The quilt is divided into fifteen pictorial rectangles, the cutout images applied to the blue cotton backing. There is outline quilting around the motifs and random intersecting straight lines in open spaces. A one-inch border of straight-grain printed cotton is folded over the edges and stitched through all layers. The batting is composed of raw, unprocessed cotton."

Liz Ridenour had been asked to say a few words about the *Shooting Star Quilt* at the opening of the Madison Meteorite Exhibit, for Lizzie was in line to head up the new Quilting Museum in the space across town where the Historical Society used to be located. Another grant from the Hoople Quadruplets Foundation. The town's famous quads would live on in the building's new name, The Hoople Quilting Heritage Museum.

Dr. Archimedes L. Claypool would be the main speaker for the Madison Meteorite's opening. Being this was the Bible Belt, he planned to lead off with a reference to Acts 9: 1-19, Saul's Conversion on the Road to Damascus. He would explain that the dazzling light seen by Saul of Tarsus in AD 35 was actually thought to be a fireball meteor. This startling astronomical event moved the Pharisee to change his name to Paul and become a follower of Jesus. Dr. Claypool would point out that the three Biblical descriptions of Paul's experience closely match accounts of the fiery bolide that exploded over Chelyabinsk, Russia, in 2013.

Science explaining religion.

Yes, thought Cookie, that certainly should get the attention of Rev. Durrenberger and his flock at First Mennonite Church. And it might even warrant a headline in the *Burpyville Gazette*.

Blasphemy, some might say. But word of mouth and publicity were the name of the game. If the *Gazette* wanted sensationalism, she would deliver just that.

Chapter Thirty-Nine

Treasure Hunt

Daniel Sokolowski piled into Maddy's Toyota SUV with Aggie and N'yen. Cookie was off in Burpyville getting posters. Lizzie was having her hair done again. Bootsie wasn't answering her iPhone, which probably meant she'd accidentally turned off the ringer (she did that a lot). So it was just the four of them – plus Maddy's bodyguard following behind them in the black car.

"If there *is* a treasure, the Jinks homestead is definitely the place it will be," said the antiques dealer. "I'm convinced Aggie is right about the message on the posy ring being a clue to the gold's whereabouts. It simply makes sense."

The Jinks homeplace was located on land adjacent to the old Madison farm, both parcels now owned by Boyd Aitkens. He was by far the largest landholder in the county. Watermelons were his big crop. He grew Charleston Greys and Black Diamonds, two popular varieties of picnic melons.

To get there, they drove past the field where they found the bones of Ace Jinks, took a right at the end of the fence, continued on a mile or so, then pulled up in front of a dilapidated stone building. The roof had caved in and the front porch was sagging. There was no glass left in the windows, giving the appearance of unseeing eyes. The Jinks homeplace was a husk of its former self.

Maddy and her charges climbed out of the car and

made their way through the overgrown yard. Briars pulled at their clothing as they followed the walkway. The yard had been dug up, like trench warfare on the Western Front in WWI, but foliage was threatening to take over.

"Tell me again what the message on the ring said," prompted Maddy.

"*The foundation of my home is golden*," recited the antiques dealer.

"This foundation looks like plain old rocks to me," said N'yen, squinting his eyes at the base that supported the house.

"Yes, I agree," replied Dan Sokolowski. "Let's inspect the basement and see what the foundation is like from the inside."

"Are you sure it's safe?" Maddy hesitated. The house looked as if about to collapse.

The old man shrugged. "We won't know until we go in."

"Isn't our bodyguard gonna come with us?" asked Aggie, glancing back at the black BMW parked behind Maddy's car. "I'd feel safer going into this spooky old house if Agent X-3 was with us."

"His name's Rex," N'yen corrected his cousin. "His boss gave him that silly code name. I think Mr. Hammer has read too many comic books."

"Hammer's not the man's real name," commented Maddy. "Jim Purdue checked him out before we hired Iron Fist. Dean Hammond calls it a *nom de guerre*. An assumed name. I suspect he was inspired by Mickey Spillane's Mike Hammer books."

"Makes sense," said N'yen. "Early in his career

Mickey Spillane wrote for comic books."

"How do you know that?" asked Maddy.

"I read."

~ ~ ~

The floorboards were rotten, but by stepping on beams they made it to the cellar door. "Careful now," said Dan Sokolowski, "These steps may be dangerous. You and the children wait here while I go down and take a close-up look at the foundation."

Maddy nodded. "Okay. Here's the Maglite. Hope you see something golden, like the ring says."

The old man proceeded down the stairwell cautiously, one step at a time, testing his weight before advancing to the next. A slender physique, he tipped the scales at less than 160 pounds; nonetheless the wooden steps creaked under his weight. His hand gripped the railing, steadying himself and taking up some of the weight. The footsteps became muffled as he descended into the depths of the basement. The house had thick walls and insulated flooring.

Maddy and the kids lingered anxiously at the cellar door. The house smelled of decay and dead mice. The light was dim, except for a shaft of sunlight that came through a hole in the roof. Time seemed to pause as they waited for the elderly antiques dealer to announce his findings. Everything was as motionless as a still life.

"Stop where you are," came a childlike voice. "You're trespassing!"

Maddy turned to face Dub Crackleton. The dwarfish man didn't look very intimidating until you noticed the German Luger griped firmly in his hand. The pistol was probably a war souvenir he'd bought off a customer. "No, we're not," she replied nervously. "Boyd Aitkens gave us permission to come out here. He owns this property."

"Oh yeah? This is the Ferdinand Jinks homeplace and I'm a direct descendant, so this property is rightfully mine no matter what the deed says. And anything you find here belongs to my family."

"Which family's that – the Crackletons or the Jinkses?"

"Granny Crackleton was a Jinks before she married our Grandpa – God rest his soul. That makes the Crackletons closer related than Fatty Johnson and his folks."

Granny was a Jinks. How did Cookie miss that in her genealogy charts? That meant Granny was – what? – the niece of Ace Jinks, that missing boy. No wonder she knew the story. Beau Madison III didn't have to confide in her; she was already clued in.

"You're saying anything we find here belongs to your family. What did you have in mind – gold?"

"Granny should never have told you that story. But the ol' biddy's getting senile. We been hunting that treasure most our life."

"Found anything?"

"Just spiders and cobwebs. But it's gotta be here someplace. Like the ring says, *The foundation of my home is golden.*"

"How do you know what the ring says? It has been buried with Ace Jinks for over a hundred years."

"Ferdinand had three boys – Ferdinand Junior, Stanton, and Ace. He gave all three identical rings. Granny was Stanton's daughter. His ring passed to her.

She keeps it in a cigar box on her nightstand."

"What are you going to do with that pistol. If the plan is to scare us off, consider yourself successful. We'll leave."

"No, you know too much now. I'll have to shoot you all and bury you in the basement. Nobody will find you. Only we Crackleton brothers come out here looking for the treasure."

"Did you have anything to do with Mycroft's death?"

"Not me. My brothers took care of that. The brakes on your son Bill's car too. They drove to Chicago. I tried to drop the cement block on your husband's head, but I wasn't tall enough to get it over the bridge railing with any aim. And I whipped up that bomb at the fire department, but your little Chink there screwed that up with his robot."

"Hey, I'm not a Chink," complained N'yen. "I'm Vietnamese, not Chinese."

"One's the same as the other," the dwarf said. "You're all slant eyes."

"Says you – you pint-sized man."

"Shut up, you little brat. Time to go down in the basement-t-t-t-t–" His words sputtered as 50,000 volts of electricity from Agent X-3's Taser raced through his diminutive body.

While Dub Crackleton was threatening them, N'yen had pressed the speed dial on the iPhone in his pocket. He'd programmed in Rex Blouderman's cell-phone number. He'd rigged a message through his voice mail that said, "Help! This is N'yen. I need your big muscles."

Better to be safe than sorry, N'yen's Uncle Võ had taught him. Be an American, but think like a Viét Minh. Good advise in his opinion.

Rex Blouderman hadn't seen Dub sneak in from

the back of the house, but the second he got N'yen's message he was out of his SUV and racing toward the house like the running back he used to be in college. Iron Fist Enterprises didn't allow its agents to carry guns – too much potential liability – but each was armed with a Pulse Taser. X-3 kept his fully charged, dutifully plugging it in every night along side his iPhone. The prongs hit the little man square between the shoulder blades, incapacitating him instantly.

Dub lay there on the dirty wooden floor, jerking and twisting like someone undergoing an epileptic seizure. Maddy reached down and delicately picked up the Luger with two fingers. "Well, that takes care of that," she said. "Looks like Iron Fist was a good investment.

~ ~ ~

N'yen went down to the cellar to check on Daniel Sokolowski. In his eighties, the old man was hard of hearing and had missed the ruckus upstairs. "Hey, Mr. Soko-whatever. You okay?"

"Over here," the old man called. "I've been examining this house's foundation, stone by stone. Nothing out of the ordinary, I'm sorry to say."

"Hard to see anything with just a flashlight," the boy responded. He played the beam of his Ray-o-vac over the subterranean room. Dirt floor, stone walls, empty shelves.

"Unfortunately, there is nothing to see. Agnes's idea was intriguing, but this may have turned out to be a wild goose chase."

"Maybe we're not reading the clue right," countered N'yen. "*The foundation of my home is golden* might simply be an admonition that they stay a close-knit family."

Aggie had come down the stairs behind her cousin. "No, dummy," she said, "If it were that, Dub and his brothers wouldn't have spent all these years searching for the treasure. He just told us they come out here and dig."

"Dummy?" N'yen couldn't believe she had called him that. Nobody ever questioned his intelligence.

The old man's flashlight bobbled. "Dub Crackleton just told you that?" exclaimed the antiques dealer. "Is he up there?"

"Yes, but Agent X-3 has him in cuffs. He threatened to shoot us."

"That little man is a *paskudneh. Eyn umglik iz far im veynik.*"

"If you say so," nodded N'yen, as if he understood Yiddish. He was still smarting over his cousin's remark.

"Dub scared me," admitted Aggie. "He said he was going to kill us and bury us here in the cellar where no one would ever find us."

"Hmm," said the old man, "that's pretty serious. We must be onto something. But I cannot figure out what."

"That wagonload of gold has to be buried around here," insisted Aggie.

"Buried?" said N'yen. "Did anyone ever dig up this cellar floor?"

As it happened, the Crackletons had. That's where the deputies later found the bodies of the inquisitive writer and a couple other "intruders" the Crackletons had spotted from their shack in the woods.

CHAPTER FORTY

Bad Foot

The phone call from Doc Medford caught Jim Purdue off guard. "Just saw something you might oughta know about," reported the physician (cum coroner). "One of Jeb Crackleton's boys came in with an injured foot. Three puncture wounds in the *plantar aponeurosis*. That's the fibrous connective tissue on the bottom of the foot. The wounds were getting infected or he wouldn't have come in."

"His foot?"

"Right. That is, his right foot. You said to be on the lookout for any foot injuries."

"Yeah, Beau Madison's grandson set up a trap for burglars. Kind of like punji sticks."

"Well, that could account for these injuries."

"Which boy was it – El or Vis. Doubt it was that dwarf Dub."

"Said his name was Vis. But you can't tell those boys apart by sight."

"Was El with him?"

"No, just the one. He left about fifteen minutes ago. Limping pretty bad. I cleaned out the wounds, bandaged it up, gave him some antibiotics and a prescription for pain pills. He's probably headed for the pharmacy at the Food Lion."

"Thanks, Doc. Anything else on those bones?"

"Oh, the bones. Sent off the DNA. Should get a

profile back in a few days. Anybody to compare it to?"

"Those Quilters Club gals – my wife included – think it's one of ol' Ferdinand Jinks's sons. Guess we could compare it to one of his ancestors – Fatty Johnson maybe."

"Get me a swab and we'll run it."

~ ~ ~

Deputy Pete Hitzer picked up both El and Vis at the pharmacy department of Food Lion. He waited till Vis got his painkillers, then brought them both to the station.

Chief Purdue was waiting. "Hello, boys. Does Jebediah know you've been killing people? Or at least trying to."

"Who – us?" said El, the one not limping.

"Got you dead to rights, excuse the expression. We can match your brother's DNA with the blood left on those pencils at the back stoop of the Madison house. It's a miracle what you can do with forensic science these days."

"Yeah, I watch CSI," said Vis. "Guess you got me. But you can't prove El had anything to do with it."

"You'll do. The murder of Mycroft Madison should be good for a life sentence."

"Wait a minute. You can't prove any of that. I'll plead guilty to attempted burglary, nothing else."

"Got a fingerprint on that bag of rocks you used to coldcock Mycroft Madison," Jim Purdue lied. "Bet it matches you."

"Ha! Got you there. My fingerprints can't be on that bag. It wasn't me who hit that queer in the head; it was El."

"Watch it!" his brother smacked him on the shoulder. "You just told him I did it."

"Oops. Didn't mean to say that."

Chief Purdue shook his head. "You boys are Crackletons alright."

EPILOGUE

Wrapped Up with a Bow

All ended well. Everything wrapped up in a bow, as Maddy liked to say.

Sure, Drake Hammer was bummed that his agent had captured one of the bad guys, thus ending this cushy four-grand-a-day assignment. But he forced a smile as the police chief shook his hand and congratulated him on what a fine job his men – particularly Rex Blouderman – had done.

Agent X-3 had likely saved Maddy and the children's lives. Being a modest guy, he took an embarrassed "Aw shucks" attitude about it. His boss reluctantly gave him a bonus.

All three of Jebediah Crackleton's sons were arrested for murder and conspiracy to commit murder. The prosecutor predicted long jail sentences for each of them. Jeb himself escaped charges, because there was no evidence of his involvement and his boys weren't about to blow the whistle on their dad. But everyone knew he was the mastermind behind this mayhem.

Granny Crackleton admitted it was all a Jinks family vendetta against the Madison and Caruthers families. The resentment went all way back to the naming of the town. But Granny wasn't judged sane enough to be believed in a court of law.

El and Vis confessed they had killed Mycroft Madison in error, mistaking him for his brother Beau.

The body of a freelance writer named Carl

Bernstein was found buried in a corner of the Jinks homeplace's cellar. Dub Crackleton owned up to it. His brothers had reported an intruder and he took care of it. In fact, Dub admitted he was responsible for a couple of more John Does buried in the cellar. Nobody was going to steal the treasure out from under them, he stated defiantly.

The gold was never found. Daniel Sokolowski reluctantly concluded the ring's message was simply a homily about the virtues of a good home life; not a treasure map. Everybody agreed that there had never been a wagonload of gold except in the warped imagination of the Crackleton clan.

A *bobbemyseh*, Sokolowski called it. An old wives tale.

The Quilters Club finished their community Quilt just in time, presenting it to Willamina Haney a week before she passed away. She put up a fight, but the Big C finally got her. Big Bill thanked them for making his wife's passing more endurable.

Fatty Johnson got his ersatz statue of Ferdinand Jinks erected in the town square. No one recognized an obscure congressman named Lincoln Dixon. Big-Nose Evans got arrested for peeing on it. He paid only a $30 fine, being Judge Cramer was sympathetic. Turns out, the judge was a Caruthers somewhere in his family tree.

Eggie Ettelman got two years in Terre Haut. Lifting weights, he'd pumped himself up. There was something to be said for a free vacation, courtesy of Uncle Sam. He planned to turn down a parole when it came time for his review.

The Madison Meteorite Exhibit was a big success, although some churchgoers objected to Archie Claypool's Biblical references. Lizzie got her appointment as director of the Hoople Quilting Heritage Museum. Bootsie lost 7 pounds on the Weight Watcher's Diet. Police Chief Jim Purdue started eating more meals at the Cozy Café to avoid the mail-order food. Maisie Walters appreciated the increased business, although she didn't need the money. Turns out, she put up the dough for a new animal shelter on the outskirts of town. Another Hoople trust fund at work.

Aggie started dating Bobby Elwood, the boy who had asked her to the prom last year. Tilly thought she was too young, having just turned fifteen, but Mark the Shark okayed it with some strict ground rules. After all, she was wearing lipstick.

N'yen thought he might have discovered a new star with his Celestron AstroMaster 114EQ. He was waiting for confirmation from the Department of Astronomy at the University of Indiana Bloomington.

Beau and his fishing buddy Edgar Ridenour were bummed that the boy had hooked Big Calvin in the water under the Highway 101 Bridge. They weighed the chucklehead at 35.7 pounds, then released him back into his murky habitat.

Maddy Madison started a new quilt, a simple Amish pattern called the Nine Patch, one that allowed her to take it easy, giving her plenty of time to think. The Quilters Club had moved its meeting place from the Hoosier State Senior Recreational Center to the new Hoople Quilting Heritage Museum. There, they had their own workroom, one which they didn't have to share with that stupid macramé club at the rec center. Aggie said the new facility was "way cool." N'yen just shrugged.

The Watermelon Days festival would be coming up in a few months and they would soon start working on their entries for this year's quilting competition. Always quite a challenge, beating last year's quilts.

But Maddy had something else on her mind. The Jinks gold.

She knew where to find it.

Thank you for reading.

Please review this book. Reviews help others find New Pulp Press and inspire us to keep providing these marvelous tales.

If you would like to be put on our email list to receive updates on new releases, contests, and promotions, go to AbsolutelyAmazingEbooks.com and sign up.

Bonus

By going to the Absolutely Amazing eBooks online website (AbsolutelyAmazingEbooks.com) and entering the password below into the Bonus Reward Section, you can access recipes for many of the dishes you read about in this book – for free!

AA1057

About the Author

Marjory Sorrell Rockwell says needlecraft arts — quilting, crocheting, knitting — are pastimes every woman can appreciate. And she particularly loves quiltmaking. "It's like painting with cloth," she says. But when not quilting she writes mysteries about a Midwestern sleuth not unlike herself, a middle-aged lady with an unpredictable family and loyal friends. And she's a big fan of watermelon pie.

ABSOLUTELY AMA⚡ING eBOOKS

AbsolutelyAmazingeBooks.com
or AA-eBooks.com

CONSTRUCTING

SOULS OF CHICAGO #5

ANNABELLA MICHAELS

Constructing the Soul
Souls of Chicago Series #5

Copyright © 2017 Annabella Michaels

ISBN: 978-0-9989888-4-9

annabellamichaels.blogspot.com

Cover art provided by Jay Aheer of Simply Defined Art – www.jayscoversbydesign.com

Editing provided by Pam Ebeler of Undivided Editing – www.undividedediting.com

Proofreading provided by Judy Zweifel of Judy's Proofreading – www.judysproofreading.com

Interior Design and Formatting provided by Stacey Blake of Champagne Formats – www.champagneformats.com